THE ~~~~
Unl

JULIET CAROLAN

THE BOOK OF SHADOWS
BY JULIET CAROLAN

Dedication

To the memory of my dear friend, Gillian Benson, whose warmth, wisdom, and unwavering support illuminated my life and inspired the pages within.

Though you left us on April 10th, 2020, your spirit continues to guide every word, making this journey both a tribute and a celebration of the profound impact you had on my world.

In loving memory and eternal gratitude.

Acknowledgment

I would like to express my deepest gratitude to my gorgeous husband Eddie, for his unwavering support, patience, and countless hours of encouragement throughout this writing process. His belief in me and his endless patience have been my greatest blessings.

I also want to thank my son Oliver for his encouragement and support, which has meant the world to me.

Without their love and understanding, this book would not have been possible.

Synopsis

In the quaint Hamlet of Harrop Fold, in a cottage named Elders Rest, two women, separated by centuries, are bound by a haunting legacy.

In 1612 Agnes Thornton, a healer accused of witchcraft, faces a storm of persecution that alters the course of Elders Rest forever. As she confronts a zealous Witch Finder, a tragic act seals her fate within the very cottage where she once brought solace. Rose, her daughter, accused unfairly, faces the wrath of an unforgiving society.

In 2023 Jess, reeling from the loss of her best friend and her bistro, inherits Elders Rest cottage from her grandmother. Unbeknownst to her, the echoes of Agnes's torment linger within the ancient walls, and the legacy of persecution resurfaces. Jess unravels the mysteries of Elders Rest through a cryptic recipe book that bridges the gap between centuries when she experiences vivid visions unlocking the secrets buried within the book.

The Book of Shadows is a tale of love, loss, and the macabre dance between the living and the departed. Can Jess free Agnes's spirit and unveil the truth that has remained hidden for centuries?

As the past whispers its secrets, the destiny of Elders Rest unfolds in a symphony of echoes that transcends the boundaries of time.

- All Recipes mentioned will be printed at the end of the book **(+)**

Table of Contents

Prologue

Chapter One
Chapter Two
Chapter Three
Chapter Four
Chapter Five
Chapter Six
Chapter Seven
Chapter Eight
Chapter Nine
Chapter Ten
Chapter Eleven
Chapter Twelve
Chapter Thirteen
Chapter Fourteen
Chapter Fifteen
Chapter Sixteen
Chapter Seventeen
Chapter Eighteen
Chapter Nineteen
Chapter Twenty
Chapter Twenty-One
Chapter Twenty-Two
Chapter Twenty-Three
Chapter Twenty-Four
Epilogue

This is a work of fiction. Names, characters, businesses, places, events, and incidents are either the products of the author's imagination or used in a fictitious manner. Any resemblance to actual persons, living or dead, or actual events is purely coincidental.

Copyright © 2024 by Juliet Carolan. All rights reserved.

Prologue
1612

Rose sat in her cold dank prison cell, her heart heavy with the weight of impending doom. The stone walls, rough and unforgiving, seemed to close in on her, suffocating her hopes and dreams. She glanced out of the narrow-barred window, catching a glimpse of the world beyond, a world she would soon have to leave behind.

Her red hair, once vibrant and flowing like a fiery river, now hung limp and lifeless around her tear-stained face. Her eyes used to sparkle with mischief and curiosity but were now clouded with sorrow and resignation. Her wrists bound by iron chains bore the scars of her cruel confinement.

The events that had led to this dark cell seemed like a blur. Accusations of witchcraft had been flung at her like poisoned arrows, fueled by fear and superstition. Her neighbors' whispers once friendly and warm, now dripped with suspicion and malice. Rumors had spread like wildfire, twisting her innocence into a damning web of lies.

As she sat in the suffocating silence of her cell, memories flooded her mind. She remembered the whispers of the wind as it caressed the tall grasses on Pendle Hill, the ancient trees standing as silent witnesses to the secrets held within their roots. She recalled the taste of wild berries on her tongue, their sweetness a reminder of the bountiful gifts' nature offered.

But amidst the memories, there lingered a haunting question. What had become of her mother? Agnes had vanished on that fateful night when the accusations had flown like venomous arrows. Rose's heart ached for the woman who had raised her, for the wisdom and love that had been snatched away so mercilessly.

In the darkness of her cell, Rose clutched a worn piece of parchment. It was a fragment of her mother's journal, filled with cryptic symbols and ancient incantations, recipes, and potions. She had discovered it lying on the floor in Elders Rest, a precious relic connecting her to the woman she had lost.

As she traced her fingers over the faded ink, Rose felt a strange surge of energy coursing through her veins. The presence of her mother lingered on that small piece of parchment, an unseen force guiding her. She could almost hear Agnes's voice whispering in her ear, urging her to seek the truth, to uncover the secrets that had led to their tragic fate.

Though the world outside her cell may see her as a condemned witch, Rose knew she possessed a strength and resilience that could not be extinguished. In the face of her imminent death, she vowed to fight for justice, to ensure that the truth would prevail.

As the final rays of sunlight faded from her cell, Rose closed her eyes, embracing the ethereal presence that enveloped her. She would face her destiny with unwavering courage and could only pray that when the end came, it would be swift and painless.

And so, in the shadows of her prison, Rose awaited her fate with a heavy heart but a determination to root out the truth and clear both herself and her mother's names.

As she saw the sunrise through the small window, she heard footsteps and voices approaching her cell door. She looked up as the heavy door swung open ....

CHAPTER ONE
2023

Harrop Fold was a tiny hamlet located three miles from Bolton-By-Bowland and situated within the Forest of Bowland. This area, also known as Bowland Fells and formerly Chase of Bowland was an area of outstanding natural beauty. The landscape was one of grandeur and isolation. The area was dominated by deeply incised gritstone fells and vast tracks of heather-covered moorland. There were steep-sided valleys that opened out into rich green lowlands, well-wooded and dotted with picturesque stone-built farms and villages. The lower slopes were crisscrossed by dry stone walls and overlooked by the omnipresent Pendle Hill.

Jess stood at the gate of Elders Rest, her heart pounding with a mixture of anticipation and nostalgia. The quaint cottage still retained the charm of a bygone era. Moss-kissed stones, weathered by the passage of time, created a picturesque façade that spoke of the cottage's rich history. A climbing rose in full bloom weaved its way around the entrance, adding a touch of vibrant colour, and the small, mullioned windows gleamed in the sunlight.

The cottage had a large garden that went all the way around it with a variety of herbs and flowers in bloom. A cobblestone path meandered through the greenery, leading visitors to the welcoming entrance with a large rustic wooden door.

Jess's full name was Jessamine a name of Persian origin, meaning Jasmine. Her mother, widowed at an early age, had become something of a traveler, hence the slightly exotic name and Jess had been raised by her grandmother Mary. Standing at an average height with a slender, athletic build Jess moved with graceful confidence. Her long blonde hair, cascading in loose waves, framed a face adorned with hazel eyes that reflected a depth of emotion. A smattering of freckles across her nose added a touch of youthful charm, and her warm smile lit up her features. Her childhood had been defined by the idyllic simplicity of rural life, the memories of meandering through fields and exploring the lush landscapes that surrounded her home. Her Lancashire roots instilled in her a sense of pride for her heritage.

An unexpected passion for the culinary arts, encouraged by her grandmother, emerged in Jess during her teenage years. Inspired by the flavours and traditions of Lancashire cuisine, she began experimenting with recipes, eventually developing a talent for crafting dishes that spoke to the heart of her cultural roots.

Life, however, was not without its challenges. Financial constraints posed obstacles, but Jess's resilience and tenacity propelled her forward and she realized her dream of creating a space where her love for cooking could be shared when she opened her Bistro in Skipton with her best friend Grace. Jess was also looking forward to catching up with her friends Adeline and Melissa. She had known Adeline since school and although they didn't talk as often as she would have liked they had always kept in touch, whilst she had met Melissa when she moved onto the same cul-de-sac in Clitheroe, where she had also met Grace. Melissa was a renowned hairdresser with her salon, whilst Adeline worked as a theatre nurse within the NHS. They were great friends and she resolved to get together with both as soon as she was settled. Her other good friend and neighbour Jeanette was away on a world cruise but they kept in touch and she would see her when she returned.

The late afternoon sun cast a warm golden glow over the landscape, illuminating the quaint stone walls of the cottage. Ivy climbed along the sides, reaching toward the heavens as if seeking to touch the clouds. A gentle breeze rustled through the ancient trees, whispering secrets of the past.

Jess's grandmother, Mary, had always held a special place in her heart. As a child, she had spent countless hours exploring the village with her, discovering nooks and crannies, listening to tales of old, immersing herself in the enchantment of the little hamlet and all the surrounding villages that lay under the watchful eye of Pendle Hill.

Taking a deep breath, Jess pushed open the creaky gate and walked up the cobblestone path that led to the cottage's front door. The scent of wildflowers wafted through the air, mingling with the earthy aroma of the surrounding countryside. It was a fragrance that instantly transported her back to her carefree days of innocence.

As she reached the door, her fingers trembling with a mix of excitement and trepidation, Jess hesitated for a moment before turning the weathered brass handle. As she glanced up at the windows upstairs, she saw a fleeting shadow pass by one of the small bedroom windows. Were the cleaners still there? Or it was Frank, her neighbour doing a last-minute check?

She opened the door and stepped in. As she gazed around, she could see the large inglenook fireplace with the newly installed wood burner her grandmother had insisted on buying, which looked as if it had never been used. She could still smell the lavender and rosemary that her grandmother used to grow on the kitchen windowsill, and it still had that comforting smell of home. She shouted to see if anyone was there but there was only silence. She must have imagined it she thought, maybe it had just been the sun reflecting off the glass.

Inside, exposed wooden beams crisscrossed the ceiling. The large fireplace dominated the room and the interior was a lovely mix of antique furniture and modern touches that merged discreetly, like the soft lighting fixtures and comfortable well-worn armchairs.

A large grandfather clock stood tall in a corner and normally marked the passage of time with its steady ticking. Jess noticed it was silent as if time had stopped when her beloved grandmother had passed. She made a mental note to ask Frank if he knew of anyone who could look at it.

As she moved through to the kitchen, she could still smell the aroma of baking, sugar and flour, vanilla, and savory spices. She looked with fondness at the old farmhouse table that had seen many hours of creation and love and laughter and the shared memories of cooking and eating.

She sat down on one of the wing-backed chairs in the sitting room and closed her eyes. The past year had been nothing short of horrendous. She had lost her best friend suddenly along with the bistro that they had both been running for 5 years due to the pandemic of 2020. Without Grace and the steady flow of customers, the bistro simply could not survive. She had been thinking for some time that she would visit her grandmother and stay and recuperate but had not anticipated yet another loss. Mary had been 87 and always in good health but a fall had resulted in a broken hip and unfortunately, she never came out of the hospital but simply passed away quietly with Jess by her side. She was shattered both in mind and body and was not even sure if she had the strength to continue but somehow, just sitting in the cottage brought her some sort of comfort and maybe even a glimmer of hope.

Suddenly she opened her eyes and looked around. She could hear scratching sounds coming from the kitchen or at least the back of the cottage. Hurriedly she ran back towards the kitchen and there on the windowsill was a little black cat, pawing at the window and mewing.

"Oh, my goodness, Bella, how could I have forgotten "Jess quickly opened the window and let the cat in. Her grandmother Mary had acquired Bella when, as a tiny kitten, she appeared one winter's morning mewing outside and she had been with her ever since, a constant companion.

"I thought Frank was looking after you," said Jess as she stroked the now-purring cat. "Come on let's get you some food". As she followed Bella towards a cupboard in the kitchen, she felt some sort of relief. At least I am not completely alone, she thought, someone needs me even if it is only Bella.

There was a knock on the door and Jess opened it to find Frank standing there. Frank lived at Higher Harrop Fold Farm, opposite Elder's Rest. Born and bred in Harrop Fold, Frank's life was a testament to the enduring connection he shared with the hamlet. His familial ties stretched across generations, making him a respected figure within the local community.

Frank's childhood had also been a tapestry of adventures in the idyllic landscapes of Harrop Fold. His path had intersected with that of Mary, Jess's grandmother, in the halcyon days of their youth. Their friendship had blossomed amidst shared laughter, secrets, and the camaraderie forged in the close-knit community.

Frank, known for his various roles in the community, had contributed to the well-being of Harrop Fold, whether it was through his work, participation in local events or simply offering a helping hand to neighbours. He also ran the local chapel which was just down the lane from the main hamlet. Every Sunday at 2 pm, villagers would come to the chapel to listen to whoever was preaching that day and afterward would stay on and share food that had all been cooked by themselves. Frank organized all the food and the preachers and even played the piano at some of the meetings. Mary had been a great contributor to the food and Frank was hoping that Jess might get involved too given her talents.

"Ah, you have found Bella I see. She has been missing since Mary passed, I have been wondering where she was" Frank bent down to stroke the little cat. "

"She has just appeared, sitting on the windowsill outside the back door. She seems ok, how long has she been missing"?

"Quite a few days, I have been looking for her and calling for her. Seems she was waiting for you to arrive Jess "Frank chuckled. "How have you been since the funeral?

"I'm ok Frank. I've given up the lease on the house in Clitheroe and closed the Bistro. I just need to think about what to do now, but I'm glad I'm here, thanks. Jess smiled at Frank.

"Well, everyone at Harrop Fold is pleased you are here too, and if there is anything I can do you know you only have to ask" Frank leaned forward and hugged Jess.

Jess hugged him back "Thank you so much. I know this may sound a bit silly but the grandfather clock doesn't seem to be working and I miss the sound. Grandma loved that clock. Do you know of anyone who might be able to look at it "Jess enquired.

"Yes, as it happens there is a new chap who just moved into the area, Philip Robinson, and I do believe he has a clock business of some sort in Slaidburn. Would you like me to ask him and see if he can come and look at it?"

"Oh yes please, if it's no trouble, thanks.", Jess replied. Suddenly there was a loud crash from upstairs that made them both jump. Bella hissed and arched her back, as Jess set off up the stairs.

As Jess got to the top of the staircase, she could see that a picture had fallen off the wall. As she picked it up, she saw that it was an old recipe that had been framed, presumably by her grandmother, although she didn't remember seeing it before. It was a very old recipe for something called Malkin Pie. (+) As she studied the recipe, something stirred within her, and she felt excited for the first time in ages. I need to get back in the kitchen, she thought. I want to try and make this pie, although looking at some of the ingredients it's going to need some updating.

"How on earth did that fall off the wall" Frank was right behind her at the top of the stairs, let me find a hammer and I'll put it back up for you."

"No, it's fine, I want to study the recipe first. Have you ever heard of Malkin Pie Frank "Jess enquired.

Frank thought for a moment, "Aye, it is believed it was a recipe that was used by the

Lancashire Witches. Do you know old Agnes Thornton used to live in this cottage? She and her daughter were accused of witchcraft, but Agnes disappeared before the trial, it's always been a big mystery around here. No one knows what happened to her, and the only records of her daughter Rose, show that she was to be tried as a Witch but nothing to say whether she was one of the witches that were hanged at Lancaster."

"Yes, my grandmother told me some stories, but I didn't know that about Agnes. I will need to find out more. Poor Rose, those were terrible times, I remember Grandmother telling me some tales. I wonder if there are any more old recipes around, like this one?"

"I'll bet there is somewhere as Mary did make some amazing pies and pastries and she liked to make the old traditional Lancashire recipes; I know that. Look, I'll leave you to get on and I'll contact Philip. If he is free, shall I just tell him to come on up to the cottage?" Frank said as he was leaving, and Jess nodded her confirmation.

Frank left with a wave and Bella followed him, making Jess laugh. Cats were a law unto themselves, and she watched the pair walk down the path and across to Frank's house. She knew Bella would be back later when she was hungry and wanted a nice warm place to sleep.

Jess went to bed that night comfortable but cold. She hadn't been able to get the wood burner in the fireplace to work, another thing she would have to ask Frank about. Although there was an Aga in the kitchen the wood burner heated the rest of the cottage.

As she lay in bed, she still could not believe she had lost her beloved grandmother and her best friend in the space of a year. She knew she was in the right place to heal and that it would take time. Much later, she heard Bella padding up the stairs and smiled as the cat settled herself on the end of the bed, purring softly, with one eye open.

Chapter Two
1612

In the early 17th century England was undergoing a period of momentous change with the transition from the Tudor era to the Stuart dynasty marking a time of political and social upheaval. There was a lot of unrest and religious persecution with the fear of witchcraft prevalent amongst the Lancashire hills.

In the countryside, life revolved around agriculture with most families relying on farming for their livelihood. The fields surrounding Harrop Fold were the scene of sheep, cows, and pigs grazing in the meadows providing essential resources like wool, milk, and meat.

But life in rural Lancashire was far from idyllic. Disease and famine were constant threats with outbreaks of the plague ravaging communities and poor harvests leading to food shortages. Superstition and fear permeated daily life, with beliefs in witchcraft and the supernatural shaping the attitudes of the villagers. The quaint hamlet of Harrop Fold nestled snugly in the rolling hills of this countryside and time seemed to move at a more leisurely pace. Cobblestone streets wound their way past centuries-old cottages, their stones and slated roofs weathered by the passage of time. At the edge of the hamlet stood Elders Rest, a modest cottage with mullioned windows that gazed out onto the surrounding fields. Smoke lazily curled from its chimney, a comforting sign of warmth and life within.

Inside the cottage dwelled Agnes a woman of gentle demeanor and quiet strength. Her weathered hands bore the mark of countless hours spent tending to herbs and concocting remedies for ailments both mundane and mysterious. Life in Harrop Fold followed the rhythms of nature, each day marked by the rising and setting of the sun. Agnes, widowed at an early age, had shouldered the burden of providing for her family alone. Her husband's passing had left a void in her heart but it had also ignited a fierce determination to carve out a future for herself and her daughter. Her husband Richard had been a farmer but he had caught a fever which turned out to be consumption and he had slowly and agonizingly passed away one Spring. This had made Agnes more determined than ever to learn all she could about herbs and their healing powers.

For women like Agnes widowhood brought not only grief but also newfound responsibilities. Without a husband to provide for them, widows often had to rely on their skills and resourcefulness to support them and their families. Agnes, with her knowledge of herbal remedies and midwifery, found a niche in the community as a healer, offering aid to those in need.

Rose, her daughter growing up in this turbulent time inherited her mother's resilience and curiosity. The village was a tight-knit community where everyone knew each other's business and rumours spread like wildfire. Although Rose learned a lot from her mother about herbal remedies and the art of midwifery, she had been lucky to secure a position at Harrington Hall in the village of Downham as a housemaid and she loved her job. As Agnes and Rose went about their daily routines they were surrounded by the sights, sounds, and smells of rural Lancashire in 1612.

As for Rose, she possessed a curious spirit and a thirst for knowledge that often led her into mischief. With her long red hair and unusual eyes, one green and one brown, she was well known in the village. Agnes watched over her with a mixture of pride and concern, knowing the world beyond their village held both wonders and dangers.

But life in Harrop Fold was not without its challenges. Superstition and the fear of the unknown hung heavy in the air, casting a shadow over their hamlet and the surrounding villages. Rumours of witchcraft and dark forces lurked in the minds of the villagers, fueled by ignorance and suspicion. Agnes, with her knowledge of herbal remedies and unconventional practices often found herself the subject of scrutiny and gossip. Rose worried about her mother but she remained undaunted. She was increasingly aware of the limitations placed upon her as a woman in 17th-century society. Marriage was often seen as the only viable path for women, a means of securing financial stability and social standing. Yet Rose had seen her mother coping on her own and she longed for independence and to carve out her own place in the world. She enjoyed her work at Harrington Hall and hoped that it may one day lead to something more.

It was her evening off that day and as Rose made her way to Elders Rest, her senses heightened by the gathering dusk, she caught sight of a shadowy figure lurking among the trees. A fleeting glimpse, barely more than a whisper in the fading light, but enough to send her heart racing and her pulse quickening.

Who was the mysterious stranger, and what did they want? Rose's mind raced with questions and with a sinking feeling in the pit of her stomach she quickened her pace, the ominous presence of the unknown looming large in her thoughts.

Little did she know this encounter would set into motion a chain of events that would alter the course of her destiny forever.

Chapter Three
2023

The next morning Jess opened the curtains in the bedroom and in the early morning light the view from the back of the bedroom was beautiful. It looked straight onto the hills behind the cottage and there amongst the trees and bracken she suddenly caught sight of three deer. As she gazed at them, one turned around and looked at her then, just as quickly it turned and in a fleeting moment had jumped a fence and was out of sight. Jess smiled, it felt like a good omen and she was looking forward to the day ahead.

Having fed Bella and made herself a cup of coffee, she was sitting in the living room when there was a knock on the door. Jess looked through the window to see a tall slim man wearing a weathered brown coat, worn from years of labour that hinted at the countless hours spent in his workshop tinkering with gears and springs. His hair was jet black and his skin sallow and grey. A wispy beard, lacking in fullness adorned his chin, its sparse strands resembling scattered tufts of dandelion fluff rather than a thick robust growth. He carried a large leather bag with various compartments and pockets carefully organized to house his array of clockmaking tools. As she glanced out of the window Jess could see a van parked that said "Philip Robinson, Master Clockmaker. She opened the wooden front door by the latch which creaked loudly as she did so.

"Hi, you must be Philip? Thanks for coming so quickly". Philip smiled but somehow Jess thought the smile didn't quite match the penetrating stare of his pale grey eyes. He exuded a kind of confidence but also an aura of menace. Jess shook her head and mentally scolded herself "This old cottage is getting to me ".

Jess took him over to the grandfather clock. "Would you like a coffee or tea?"

"Yes, thanks that would be lovely, white one sugar please. This clock is a fine example of its era. I'll have a good look and see if I can fathom out why it stopped working "Philip put his bag down and began to examine the clock. "This is a John Alker longcase clock. I've mended a few of these in my time."

Philip had lived in Burnley for most of his life but had recently moved to Slaidburn to open another shop as he had followed in the tradition of his father and had become a clockmaker. He was fascinated by timepieces and loved his work. He had never been to Elders Rest cottage before, however, when he entered and looked around the living room, he felt a sense of de-ja-vu, as if he had been here before. It was very unsettling, and he felt the beginnings of a headache. He began to feel stressed and anxious. He had not slept well the night before which he decided must be the reason for his strange reaction to being in the cottage.

Inspecting the clock with practiced precision Philip's keen eyes noticed an imperceptible seam along the frame. He was surprised as this wasn't normally present on this kind of clock. His fingers traced a hidden latch, unveiling a secret compartment.

As he opened the latch his fingers touched something hard. After some twisting and turning he pulled out an aged, leather-bound book nestled within. He extracted the book with an eerie sense of purpose, its cover bearing the faded marks of antiquity. He studied it closely and looking inside he could see recipes but also symbols and markings.

It was as if the book was hot in his hands, and he felt an irresistible urge to put it straight in his bag without telling Jess. There was a slight tear on the bottom of one of the pages and its parchment was very old and frail. He felt a sense of anticipation and excitement but also a fear of something else that he couldn't understand.

Whilst she was waiting for the kettle to boil, Jess noticed a tall, well-built man coming out of the cottage next door, Manor House. His tousled chestnut hair fell carelessly over his forehead, framing a strong jawline and deep brown eyes. He was dressed in casual trousers and t t-shirt and carrying what looked like a vintage camera. Jess didn't recognize him from her previous visits and wondered when he had moved in and how long he was staying.

The man in question was Edward Hawthorne. He was 34 and a teacher at one of the local secondary schools, Clitheroe Royal Grammar School, which was located on Chatburn Road in Clitheroe. He taught History, and his other passion was his photography. He spent hours in the countryside and surrounding villages taking pictures and generally enjoying the local history. He had recently met Frank in the local pub and consequently came to rent Manor House. He had taken the lease for a year, but he already knew that he would probably be staying a lot longer than that. He loved the cottage and the hamlet and was keen to get to know his neighbours. He had not known Mary but was sad for the young woman he had seen moving into Elders Rest, Frank had told him that she was the granddaughter and he decided to go over and introduce himself later that day.

"What's that you've found" Jess's voice suddenly made Philip jump as if he hadn't seen her coming back in with the coffee, he was so intent on staring at the book. "A hidden treasure?" he remarked, his voice low and enigmatic. Jess watched, her curiosity mingled with a growing sense of unease, as Philip perused the pages with a deliberate intensity.

"A recipe book "Philip murmured, though his words carried an unsettling weight. "Although I think this is more of a Book of Shadows." He was almost whispering to himself, and Jess's unease grew palpable, a chill racing down her spine. "What do you mean?" she asked, her voice tinged with apprehension. "These writings," Philip continued cryptically, turning a page with deliberate slowness, "whisper of powers long slumbering, of a heritage entwined with Lancashire's darkest folklore, not just recipes as it would appear," Philip replied, wondering where the words he had just spoken had come from. Jess's heart quickened as Philips's piercing gaze seemed to bore into her, stirring a sense of trepidation. His demeanor was no longer merely enigmatic-it was tinged with the unsettling aura of menace that she had felt before.

"I'll alleviate you of this burden, as I am sure it is of no interest to you". He placed the book on top of his coat looking at Jess with his intense pale stare. Jess's breath hitched, feeling a sense of danger emanating from the clock mender's intent gaze. She grabbed the book and clutched it protectively, sensing a subtle threat lingering in Phillip's insistent words.

"No" she stammered, her voice faltering but resolute. "This ... book is mine. I'll keep it." Philip's eyes bore into hers for a moment longer, a faint smirk tugging at the corners of his lips, before he resumed his work on the clock. After a while, Phillip turned to Jess "It seems to be working now. Thanks for the coffee, I'm sure I'll see you again soon." He took another look at the book, his gaze almost angry, although he still couldn't understand his feelings or where the strange words had come from.

After Jess had paid him and Philip had left the cottage, a sinister aura seemed to linger in the room, the ticking of the clock now sounding like an ominous warning. As Philip returned to his van, he couldn't understand his feelings. He had spoken words that he didn't understand, and he felt terrible anger and an almost desperation to have the book. He knew that the book had some importance to him and that he would do anything to get hold of it, but still did not understand why.

Jess sat cross-legged on the worn antique rug, leafing through the ancient recipe book. The aroma of dried herbs seemed to infuse the air as she studied the faded script of a particular recipe for "Lancashire Foots" **(+)**. Intrigued by the script's swirling strokes, Jess traced her fingers along the words, murmuring them softly under her breath. Suddenly, a jolt surged through her, causing her surroundings to blur. The lights seemed to dim, and an inexplicable coldness enveloped her although the fire suddenly came to life and crackled, casting shadows on the cottage walls.

The air quivered with an eerie silence as the cottage transformed before her eyes. No longer was she in the present; instead, she stood amidst the stone walls of a rustic 17th-century kitchen.

She could see a woman, her hair in braids with a veil or cap, wearing a plain brown shift and a jacket that was cut low and square. She could feel every tremor of the past reverberate through her bones. Panic surged within her chest, yet she was powerless to alter the course of this hauntingly vivid experience. She appeared to be preparing the very same recipe that Jess had been reading and she was glancing anxiously toward the cottage door. Fear etched lines upon her face, her eyes darting nervously, a reflection of the grim atmosphere that hung heavy in the air.

Jess could feel an overwhelming sense of foreboding, an unexplainable dread that gripped her very soul. She could hear footsteps approaching the door.

As the woman turned round, the door creaked open revealing a shadowy figure framed by the dim light of the moon.

"Agnes" the voice whispered, "They're coming for you".

Abruptly, the scene shifted back, the flames in the hearth gone, the scent of herbs had disappeared, and Jess found herself gasping for breath, clutching the recipe book tightly, the pages fluttering in her trembling hands. The taste of fear lingered in her mouth, the ghostly whispers of Agnes' dread still reverberating within her.

There was a loud banging on the door and as the handle turned, Jess screamed, and everything went black.

Chapter Four
1612

Harrington Hall stood proudly amidst the Lancashire countryside overlooked by the magnificent Pendle Hill. The imposing structure bore testament to centuries of opulence and tradition, its façade adorned with intricate half-timbering that hinted at the grandeur within. Set against a backdrop of lush sprawling grounds, the manor exuded an air of magnificence. Towering oak trees and well-manicured gardens surrounded the estate. The serenity of the village and the majesty of Pendle Hill created an idyllic setting. The village of Downham was a lovely traditional Lancashire village, with a local ale house and cottages, all owned by Lord Harrington, and a large church and vicarage. There was a traditional village green and a babbling brook running through the streets.

Rose was a junior housemaid and her first duty in the morning was to report to the housekeeper's room. Mrs. Perkins was a stern austere woman and not much liked by the other household servants, but Rose had to have her housemaid's box checked for supplies before she could begin her daily chores.

Setting to work she drew back and shook the curtains in the drawing room and cleaned the fireplaces. This was an arduous task and not one that she relished. She was expected to rake out the fireplaces and put the ashes in her housemaid's box, light the fires, wash the hearthstone, and put the coal buckets out in the hall for two footmen to collect and fill. She also took any small rugs or druggets outside to shake. At least twice a week she hand brushed the carpets and swept the floors. She had to repeat this process in the music room and the sitting rooms, of which there were three. Then there was the library and upstairs the bedrooms. Once the dust had settled, she returned to each room and vigorously rubbed the furniture using two cloths, one in each hand.

After she finished her morning tasks, she changed from her heavy grey working apron into a clean white one and set about visiting the family in their rooms to make sure they had everything they needed. Eventually, she returned to the kitchen and finally managed to sit down to eat her breakfast of bread, cheese, and ale with the other maids until it was time to go and do the polishing

***.

That morning Jane the new kitchen maid, arrived at Harrington Hall, her expression as dull as the grey clouds that hung low in the sky. Dressed in a plain, worn dress with her hair pulled back into a tight bun, she cut a stark contrast to the grandeur of the estate. As she stepped through the heavy wooden doors into the kitchen, the other servants including Rose cast curious glances in her direction. Jane paid them little mind, her gaze fixed straight ahead, she was used to the looks people gave her. She had suffered a bout of smallpox as a child and although she had survived, it had left her face pockmarked with an unhealthy pallor. It had also made Jane bitter and resentful of anyone with an unmarked pretty face and those of privilege and wealth who could afford doctors and other luxuries denied her as she grew up.

The head cook, Peggy Higgins, eyed the new arrival with a mixture of suspicion and resignation. "So, you're the new kitchen maid, are you?" she said, her voice laced with skepticism. Jane merely nodded in response; her lips pressed into a thin line. She had little patience for idle chatter, especially from those who judged her without knowing her story.

"Well let's get to work, girl we've got Roasted Sparrows and Lamprey Pies to make" (+) Peggy instructed Jane and set her to work plucking the feathers of a dozen sparrows.

For weeks, Jane kept mostly to herself, her interactions with the other servants terse and brusque. Rose tried her hardest to engage her in conversation, but Jane resented Rose's looks and cheerful disposition. She also knew that the other servants spoke in hushed tones about her past, speculating about the reasons for her abrupt departure from her previous position. She had a simmering anger that threatened to boil over at any moment. She had worked for Lord Harrington's brother over in Yorkshire, Sir Reginald Harrington but had been accused of theft and dismissed. She had cursed him and the other Harringtons and vowed to get her revenge. Luckily no one knew where she worked before and she had been lucky to secure this position. She had been delighted when she heard the news about Sir Reginald's untimely death. He had succumbed very quickly to a mysterious fever and despite the efforts of the family physicians had fallen gravely ill and died. At the time whispers of foul play had lingered in the air like a sinister fog, but only Jane knew the truth, secrets she had sworn never to reveal.

***

Upstairs amongst its vast halls, Lord Ashton Harrington reigned supreme. Tall and imposing, with a sharp countenance marked by a resolute jawline and piercing eyes of cobalt blue, he commanded attention wherever he strode. His salt-and-pepper hair spoke of wisdom earned through years of lordship, and his attire bespoke of a man of wealth and authority.

Beside him, Lady Evelyn Harrington exuded grace and elegance that matched the splendor of the manor. Her stature was regal, with porcelain skin and flowing chestnut locks that cascaded like silk down her back. The weight of her unspoken desires and burdens was evident in the furrowed lines upon her forehead, and her downcast gaze and demeanor.

Lord Harrington was a man bound by tradition, steeped in the rigid beliefs of his time. His demeanor, though noble, was marred by an air of suspicion and an unwavering aversion to anything associated with witchcraft. He carried the weight of a personal tragedy that fueled his apprehension.

An incident in his recent past when his beloved brother fell victim to what was believed to be a curse had left an indelible mark on his psyche. The mysterious circumstances surrounding his brother's demise left a deep-seated fear of the supernatural, especially the unseen forces attributed to witchcraft in those days. His fervent belief in the malevolence of witches was ingrained in him now, shaping his attitude toward any deviation from the accepted norms.

They were in the Morning Room of Harrington Hall, observing the estate with a mixture of pride and sorrow. Lord Harrington, a man driven by an unyielding determination, carried the responsibility of a lineage steeped in tradition and legacy. Lady Evelyn, a portrait of quiet resilience, yearned for an heir to secure the family line and soften the harsh edges of Lord Harrington's unwavering rule."

"Is there any word from the physicians?" Lady Evelyn's voice, soft yet tinged with worry, broke the silence that enveloped them.

Lord Harrington's gaze, fixed upon the sprawling gardens, hardened with resolve. "None that brings solace, my dear. The physicians speak in riddles, offering no reassurance."

Harrington Hall was more than a dwelling; it was a crucible of hopes and dreams, shadowed by the haunting specter of barrenness. Lord Harrington's obsession with an heir had cast a pall over the once vibrant halls, perpetuating an atmosphere laden with both longing and apprehension. The Hall bore witness to the silent struggles, etched in the stone and whispered amongst the tapestries. "Indeed, "Evelyn looked at her husband. "I've been thinking, perhaps there might be alternative remedies that could aid me in conceiving."

"Alternative remedies?" Lord Harrington's tone tightened slightly. "You mean… tonic or elixirs concocted by local women?"

"Yes", Evelyn nodded, her resolve gathering strength. "There's a woman in the village, reputed for her knowledge of herbal remedies. Some say she has helped women in our predicament before."

Lord Harrington's countenance grew stern. "My dear Evelyn, I cannot condone such practices. To seek help from someone dabbling in such superstitions, it's preposterous."

"But Ashton, if there's a chance?" Evelyn looked at him pleadingly.

"No!" His voice reverberated through the room, cutting her off sharply. "I'll not have you entertain such notions. We are seeking proper counsel, I will not turn to concoctions and witchcraft, I expressly forbid it. Furthermore, I have been discussing things with members of the local council and we are considering getting a witchfinder to visit our villages and cleanse ourselves of these women. They consort with the devil, and I am surprised you should even mention something so heinous." Lord Harrington was shouting now and red in the face. "I will see you later at dinner Evelyn, when I hope, you have come to your senses. I do not want to hear any more of this nonsense".

He stormed out of the morning room, banging the door behind him and nearly knocking Rose over who had been outside polishing the floor and couldn't help but overhear what had just transpired. She knew that there was a lot of disquiet and fear amongst the villagers with rumors of witchcraft and she feared for her mother Agnes who was known for her healing abilities. It was a time of great fear as Rose understood her mother was certainly no witch, but they had been aware for a while that some women of other villages had been accused and sent for trial or even worse drowned or burnt. She would talk to her mother at the weekend and warn her to be careful.

Evelyn sighed and gazed out of the window. She knew that her husband was adamant that there were witches and people in the village who didn't hold his strict religious views, but Evelyn wasn't convinced and was sure that the woman she had been told of was just a very knowledgeable person and she silently resolved to find out further details. She rang the bell for Winthrop the butler. Alfred Winthrop had been with Evelyn since she was a child and she had brought him with her when she married Ashton. There was no doubt where his loyalties lay, and she would question him further this morning.

Alfred Winthrop was a figure of commanding presence within Harrington Hall. Tall and dignified, he possessed a distinguished countenance marked by years of devoted service. His silver-streaked hair was impeccably groomed, framing a face line with the wisdom of experience. His eyes held a gaze that exuded both warmth and an unmistakable air of authority. Clad in the butler's uniform, a meticulously tailored black coat, waistcoat, and perfectly pressed trousers, Alfred cut a figure of utmost elegance. His movements were deliberate and precise, each step measured with the grace and poise that defined his tenure as the steward of Harrington Hall. His voice, deep and resonant, carried a tone of quiet authority that commanded respect. Alfred's demeanor was a blend of formality and genuine concern for the well-being of the household. His dedication to his duties was unwavering, and he approached every task with an exacting eye for detail.

Beyond his role as a butler, Alfred Winthrop was an embodiment of tradition and the custodian of the estate's history. He was fiercely loyal to the Harrington family, but especially Lady Harrington whom he had known as a young girl, and he was entirely devoted to her.

He knocked on the morning room door after being summoned by Lady Harrington and was surprised, on entering, when she asked him to close the door and take a seat. After she had explained what could only be described as a very delicate situation, a troubled Alfred left the morning room and went in search of Rose.

Finding Rose in the hallway arranging some flowers, he asked if she could step out into the garden as he wanted a private conversation with her. "Miss Rose", Alfred began, his tone respectful yet tinged with concern. "Might I have a word with you in private?" Rose looked at Alfred "Of course, Mr Winthrop. Is everything all right?"

"I wish to speak to you about a matter of utmost secrecy" he replied, gesturing toward a nearby bench where they could converse discreetly.

As they settled onto the bench, Alfred chose his words carefully. "It has come to my attention that Lady Harrington is seeking assistance. Her desire for an heir is weighing heavily upon her." Rose nodded, understanding the gravity of the situation. "Yes, it must be a matter of great importance to the family."

"Your mother, Agnes, "Alfred continued cautiously, "is known for her remarkable abilities. Lady Harrington is considering seeking such assistance. If there is any way she could assist in this delicate matter it could be of great help."

Rose's eyes widened with understanding, and she glanced around, ensuring their privacy. Her mother's

reputation for her healing knowledge and remedies was well-known within the village. "I'll talk to her. If there's anything that might help Lady Harrington, I'll find out".
Alfred nodded gravely. "It's crucial that this information remains confidential. Lord Harrington must not be privy to these discussions. Lady Harrington's wellbeing is of the utmost importance, but this matter requires discretion".

Rose nodded and resolved to talk to her mother when she went home. However, she also knew that she was putting her mother and herself in great danger if Lord Harrington were to discover anything about these plans. With a heavy heart, she went back to her duties, unable to quell the rise of fear within her.

Jane, who had been out to the kitchen garden to gather some vegetables for dinner that evening, overhead the conversation and smirked to herself. The knowledge of what she had learnt may well prove useful to her in the future and she returned to the kitchen already plotting her revenge.

CHAPTER FIVE
2023

Edward Hawthorne had grown up in the picturesque village of Dunsop Bridge and had spent his childhood exploring the countryside and had developed his love of photography from his long walks with his father, spotting wildlife and old ruins. After completing his studies at the prestigious University of Oxford, where he majored in history, Edward found himself drawn back to the tranquil beauty of Lancashire. Seeking a change of pace from bustling city life, he accepted a teaching position at a secondary school in Colne, before applying for the head of history at Clitheroe Royal Grammar School. He loved this area of the world and his job where he was able to share his passion for history with the next generation.

He had gone out early that morning with his trusty camera and taken the path behind the Manor House where he was staying which took him through fields and up onto the fells. He had decided that he would go and introduce himself to the girl at Elders Rest. It was a Saturday and the weather was warm and clear. He had met Frank at a local pub in Slaidburn, Called The Hark to Bounty, which had a rich history and was one of the reasons he had gone in the first place. The Inn was reputed to date back to the 1300s. The inn was known as The Dog until 1875 when the squire of the village, who was also the Rector, had a pack of hounds. One day whilst hunting he and his party had called at the inn for refreshments. Their drinking was disturbed by loud and prolonged baying from the pack of dogs outside. High above the noise of the other hounds could be heard the squire's favourite dog "Bounty", which prompted him to call out "Hark to Bounty!" and hence the name of the inn was changed.

The upstairs of the inn was an old Courtroom that dealt with local matters such as land transfer, disputes over land rights, etc. in addition to the punishment of local miscreants. Edward loved the history of the old pub and enjoyed calling in there for a pint or some food.

Manor House, the cottage he was renting was too big for him alone but it had been lovingly restored after the previous tenants had vacated and Edward loved the big kitchen and the huge inglenook fireplace in the living room. The previous tenants had been an odd couple according to Frank and he was pleased that Edward wanted to rent it long term. As he made his way back down the fells, he was looking forward to meeting Jess, as Frank had told him she was called. He had to admit to himself that along with wanting to know his neighbour, Elders Rest was situated at the back of Manor House, he had also thought she was very attractive. He had enjoyed several relationships over the years but nothing that had lasted and it would be nice to get to know her, he thought.

Edward glanced through the window of Elders Rest as he knocked loudly on the front door, and a scene unfolded that caught him off guard. His gaze fell upon Jess, lying motionless on the floor, her features pale and her brow glistening with perspiration. He quickly knocked again on the door and thankful that it wasn't locked, he pushed it open and ran into the living room.

"Hello, Jess" Edward's voice echoed through the cottage as he hurried to her side, dropping his belongings in haste. He knelt beside her, his heart pounding with concern. Gently brushing a lock of hair from her forehead, he called out her name again, hoping to rouse her from unconsciousness. Panic threatened to seize him as he checked for any signs of injury.

"Come on, wake up" he urged softly, his voice laced with worry.

Moments that felt like an eternity passed before Jess stirred, her eyelids fluttering open slowly. Confusion clouded her gaze as she attempted to focus on the concerned face hovering over her.

"Do I know you?" her voice was barely a whisper, tinged with uncertainty.

"I'm sorry, no you don't, I'm your neighbour, Edward" he reassured her, relieved to see her consciousness returning. "What happened" Are you hurt?"

Jess blinked several times, trying to gather her thoughts. I... I 'm not sure I was reading and then I was dreaming I think and then there was a knock on the door and everything went dark."

Edward's brow furrowed with concern. "Reading? Are you certain you're all, right?"

"I think so," Jess replied weakly, attempting to sit up with his assistance. "I must have passed out.

Edward helped her to a sitting position and got her a glass of water from the kitchen. Jess thanked him weakly, sipping the water and allowing herself to regain composure.

"It must have been a powerful book if reading it caused you to pass out?". Edward was looking around for the book but could only see an old, tattered notebook lying next to Jess.

"It was an old recipe book, which simply doesn't make sense" Jess replied "The whole room seemed to change, and I heard…. oh, it doesn't matter I'm sure I'm just tired after all that's happened. Thank you for helping, did you come round for something specific?" Jess didn't want to seem rude, but she wanted to be alone to process what had just happened.

"I just came round to introduce myself. I'm Edward as I said. I live at Manor House, the Cottage at the front of yours. I teach history at the local secondary school. I'd love to have a look at the old recipe book if you wouldn't mind?"

After the dealings with Philip and then the fainting, Jess wanted to just be left alone. "I'm sorry could we do this another time? I have things to do. I'm very pleased to meet you but maybe it's better if you left now?" Jess quickly picked up the book and made her way towards the door.

Edward took the hint but was worried as Jess seemed very flustered and somewhat disturbed. "Sure, no problem. You know where I am, just call round if you need anything" and he left, taking another quick look at Jess as she closed the cottage door.

***

As Jess closed the door, she took a deep breath. What had just happened? She went and sat on the sofa. If only Grace was here, was her first thought as always when she needed to talk or wanted a hug. She had lost her best friend in April of 2020, at the height of the covid infection when everyone was in lockdown.

Grace and Jess had met when Grace moved onto the cul-de-sac after she had left her husband, or rather her husband had walked out after revealing he had been having an affair. They instantly became friends and were soon very close and Jess could always tell Grace anything. It was a lovely friendship and they enjoyed spending time together.

At the time they met, Jess was working at a local café and Grace would come in most days to have a coffee and a chat. At home, they both enjoyed cooking for each other and experimenting and it was through this that, along with the help of money that Grace had received through her divorce, they set up the Bistro which they both ran and was becoming very successful. Jess herself had experienced a bitter end to a long relationship and felt this was how she and Grace had also bonded.

Unfortunately, Grace didn't settle into the single life very well and was constantly on dating websites and had been on many disastrous dates. She finally met Rob, who also owned a café and various other buildings he rented out. He lived over in Rawtenstall.

Jess disliked him on sight and having been in his company a few times she knew he wasn't a good person and certainly not right for Grace. However, she wouldn't listen and became quite obsessed with him and eventually after a couple of years moved in with him. Things didn't go as planned, and they parted after five years together. However, despite Grace moving back into the same house near Jess again, she never got over him. Along with a joint mortgage on the bistro, Grace had also invested some money into one of Rob's businesses, a hairdresser he let out. Grace always insisted that they had to remain friends because of this, but Jess always felt Rob was just controlling and Grace couldn't let go.

When covid hit, they had to close the bistro. This was in late March 2020. They had been discussing doing takeaways for collection or delivery which other cafés and restaurants were doing and had been working on menus and options.

Rob had been on a skiing trip with another woman to northern Italy and Grace had been distraught, even though they were no longer a couple. One evening when Jess was pouring over some recipes, she got a phone call from Grace to say that she was at Blackburn Royal Hospital with Rob who had tested positive for COVID-19 and had asked Grace to take him to the hospital.

Jess remembered being so angry with her. How could she be so stupid? She was supposed to be isolated and certainly not in a car with someone who possibly had the virus. Grace wouldn't listen and went so far as to let Rob stay with her until he felt better. Jess couldn't believe her stupidity and they did end up having words. They never fell out, but Jess couldn't help but be annoyed with Grace. It was so irresponsible, and she had put herself at risk.

On Thursday the 2nd of April Grace called her to say she felt ill, and she had been calling 111 for advice. Jess wanted to do all she could to help but it was so difficult because they were isolated and not supposed to meet. Jess had been very concerned about taking any possible infection to her grandmother. By the next morning, Grace was worse, and Jess begged her to call an ambulance. Eventually, she did, and Jess talked to her on her mobile telephone until she got to the hospital. The last text she got from Grace was to say that she was in intensive care as she was struggling with her breathing and the doctors were thinking of putting her on some sort of ventilator.

She called the hospital several times that day, but they wouldn't tell her anything because Grace had given Rob as the contact to call for information. Jess reluctantly got in touch with Rob and asked him to always keep her informed. Rob seemed very upset but at the same time, Jess felt he was almost gloating that Grace had chosen him over herself as the point of contact.

The call came on Friday 10th April. Having been on a ventilator for the past 5 days, Grace's organs had failed, and she passed away at 10.00 pm that night.

The news hit Jess like a shattering wave, tearing through the fabric of her world with brutal force. Grace, her confidante, the one who laughed at her jokes, wiped her tears, and shared her dreams, was gone. A virus had snatched her away, leaving behind an aching void that seemed impossible to fill.

At first, it felt surreal, as if reality had woven a cruel, twisted tapestry. Denial clung to Jess like a suffocating cloak, refusing to accept the undeniable truth. She scrolled through old messages, even leaving a message, desperately seeking a sign of Grace, a hint that this was all a mistake. But the haunting silence echoed louder than any words they'd shared.

The numbness slowly gave way to a torrent of emotions, crashing against Jess's defenses with unrelenting intensity. Grief, raw and unyielding, consumed her along with an overwhelming hatred for Rob. Each breath felt heavy as if she carried the weight of an entire world on her shoulders. Tears flowed freely, marking a path of sorrow on her cheeks.

Memories assaulted her mind, each one a bittersweet dagger. Their laughter ringing in the park, secrets shared at work and in wine bars, and the countless moments woven into the tapestry of their friendship, now a mosaic of heartache. The ache in her chest was both a testament to their bond and a relentless reminder of its sudden rupture.

Anger seethed beneath the surface, a tempestuous storm brewing within Jess. Anger at the unfairness of it all, at the relentless virus that stole Grace away, at the helplessness gnawing at her soul. The rage she felt for this senseless death and the hatred for Rob who in her mind was the one responsible. She wanted to scream at the world, to demand answers that would never come, to shake the heavens until they made sense of this senseless loss.

Loneliness became a constant companion, a shadow trailing her every step. Grace had been the one who understood her without words, who saw through the façade and embraced her flaws. Now left to navigate a world without her guiding light, Jess felt adrift in a sea of uncertainty.

But amidst the grief and turmoil, a flicker of Grace's spirit lingered, a beacon of strength and resilience. Jess vowed to honour her friend's memory, to carry forth the lessons learned, and the love shared. Though Grace was gone, her impact on Jess's life remained etched in her heart, a timeless tribute to a friendship that transcended mere existence.

***

Jess realized how rude she had been to her new neighbour but she had needed time to process what had happened. She would kill two birds with one stone, as they say. Whilst she thought things through, she would make a pie and take it over to him later as a way of an apology. She decided to make Lancashire Cheese and Onion Pie **(+)** an old favorite and one that she knew by heart.

As she headed off into the kitchen she suddenly returned to the lounge and picked up the old recipe book. She wondered if there was a recipe in there that was like hers and just out of curiosity, she began looking through the book.

There was indeed a recipe for cheese and onion pie. As she cast her eyes over the ingredients, she noticed some symbols and words that were unfamiliar, and suddenly, the atmosphere in the cottage changed again. The air grew colder, and she could smell woodsmoke and herbs. As she looked around, once again her whole world had suddenly changed.

She was looking at a market square, which bustled with life. A vibrant tapestry of colours and activities captivated her senses. Stalls adorned with vibrant banners and awnings formed a labyrinthine maze, each one boasting an eclectic assortment of goods. The air was thick with the mingling scents of spices, freshly baked bread, and the earthy aroma of herbs.

Amidst the cobbled streets, merchants proudly displayed their wares upon wooden carts and makeshift tables. Baskets overflowed with plump ripe fruits, apples, pears, and berries glistening in the sunlight. A cacophony of voices, speaking in various dialects and accents, echoed through the air as sellers called out their offers, vying for the attention of passersby.

Stalls devoted to provisions and essentials drew a crowd, as villagers bartered for flour, cheese, and cured meats. The aroma of freshly baked pies and loaves of bread wafted from nearby bakeries, enticing hungry patrons with their warm savory scent.

A troupe of minstrels, perched on a makeshift stage, regaled the crown with lively tunes played on lutes and fiddles. Their music mingled with the laughter of children, who darted between the stalls, chasing each other in playful abandon. In the middle of this busy market, she caught a glimpse of a slim girl with red hair, walking through the streets with a basket. She suddenly turned and looked straight at Jess, the penetrating gaze of her eyes seemed to stare at her with determination before she turned and disappeared into the crowd.

As soon as the vision appeared, it faded, and she was once again on her settee holding the old recipe book in her hands. She stood up shakily and made her way to the kitchen, her head still full of the sights and sounds of that market that could only have been from the 17th century or similar, something she knew nothing about, but it had been so vivid.

She decided there and then that she would talk to Edward, her new neighbour, when she took over his pie later that day. She realized that she didn't really know him but there was something about him that seemed calming and sensible and he had seen first-hand the effects of the vision she had seen.

The pie was cooling on the side and as she was washing up and looking out at the garden, she saw a fleeting image of the young girl with long red hair. Her eyes were hollow, her skin pale and she seemed to have a faint glow around her. Quicker than the blink of an eye, she vanished.

Chapter Six
Past 1612

In the rustic tranquility of Elders Rest cottage, Agnes tended to the hearth, the crackling fire casting dancing shadows on the timeworn walls. Rose entered; her footsteps muffled by the cozy rugs that lined the floor.

"Mother, may I speak with you?" Rose's voice quivered slightly, a blend of earnestness and concern.

Agnes turned from the fire, her eyes reflecting both warmth and age-old wisdom. "Of course, dear, sit."

As they settled by the hearth, Rose hesitated for a moment before broaching the weighty topic. "It's about Lady Harrington and her wish for an heir. Mr Winthrop, the butler at Harrington Hall, suggested that your knowledge might be of help to her." Rose explained, her voice tentative.

"There are remedies, however, I am quite sure Lord Harrington won't agree "Agnes's brow creased with silent contemplation.

"No, it must remain a secret. Is there anything we can do?" Rose asked eagerly, her eyes filled with hope.

Agnes took her daughter's hands, the warmth of her touch soothing. "There's an old recipe, passed down through the generations. It carries the essence of hope, but its success depends on the lady's belief and the alignment of fate. However, Rose these are troubling times, and I am not sure that our involvement in this is a good idea or even safe."

In the 17th century, suspicion veiled the air like a shroud, casting a shadow of fear upon the quaint village nestled in the heart of Lancashire. Whispers, laden with apprehension, flitted through the narrow-cobbled streets and stone-built cottages. Superstitions coiled around every corner, and the mere mention of a strange occurrence could kindle a blaze of suspicion. Witches were feared and believed to lurk in the shadows, wielding clandestine powers that could alter destinies. Unexplainable events and misfortunes became branded with the mark of witchcraft, igniting a fervor of paranoia that spread like wildfire, rendering even the most innocent actions susceptible to accusations of sorcery.

"I know Mother, but I am sure it will be all right. Mr Winthrop will help, and Lord

Harrington will never know, I promise" Rose begged her.

"Very well, child, let's begin but let us also say a prayer whilst we are doing this" Agnes replied.

Agnes and Rose gathered the necessary herbs and ingredients, arranging them meticulously upon the worn wooden table. The air was thick with anticipation mingled with a sense of caution.

"Mother, are you certain about this potion?" Rose's voice carried a hint of apprehension.

Agnes, her weathered hands expertly sorting the dried herbs, nodded with resolve.

"I have made this brew before, under similar circumstances. It's not a certainty but as I said, it carries the essence of hope".

Rose watched as Agnes began the delicate process, carefully measuring each ingredient and grinding the herbs with a practiced hand. There was Red Raspberry Leaf, Nettle, Geranium, and Hawthorn. The flickering candlelight cast elongated shadows across the worn walls, adding an air of mystery to the proceedings.

"It's the lady's belief in the potion that matters" Agnes explained softly, sensing

Rose's unease. "But this potion holds the promise of comfort, if nothing more."

As the concoction simmered over the fire, filling the room with an aromatic blend of herbs, the flames danced, casting a hypnotic glow on the faces of the women, their thoughts consumed by Lady Harrington's plight. "Will this truly help her?" Rose queried her voice a whisper in the quiet room.

Agnes glanced at her daughter, her eyes reflecting both determination and a trace of melancholy. "The workings of fate and the mysteries of life are beyond our grasp, child. We can only offer what we know and hope for the best."

With a steady hand, Agnes decanted the potion into a vial, the liquid shimmering under the candlelight. Rose watched, a mixture of hope and uncertainty swirling within her, as her mother corked the vial, sealing the potion that carried the weight of Lady Harrington's aspirations.

"Secrecy is vital," Agnes reminded Rose solemnly. "This potion must reach Lady Harrington discreetly. Together, they vowed to deliver the potion without arousing suspicion, aware of the consequences if their actions were discovered.

As the night enveloped Elders Rest in its quiet embrace, the vial containing the potion glinted faintly, holding within its confines the essence of a fragile promise that might alter the course of Lady Harrington's desires.

***

Lord Harrington paced the length of the grand hall, his brow furrowed with concern as he awaited the arrival of David Walker, the renowned witchfinder whose services he had recently engaged.

David Walker was a man of considerable repute, known throughout Lancashire for his expertise in rooting out the taint of witchcraft wherever it lay. His reputation preceded him, and Lord Harrington had spared no expense in securing his services to safeguard his household from the sinister influence of the occult.

The heavy oak doors swung open, and David Walker strode into the hall as he made his way towards Lord Harrington with purposeful strides.

"Lord Harrington," David greeted him with a curt nod, his sharp gaze sweeping over the hall and his surroundings. Lord Harrington looked at him gravely, his expression serious.

"I have spared no expense in ensuring that you have everything you need to root out any trace of witchcraft that may have infiltrated my household or the villages surrounding it, and I am ready for you to begin your investigations."

David's lips curved into a grim smile, his pale grey eyes alight with a fervent zeal for his task. "Rest assured, my lord, I shall leave no stone unturned in my pursuit of justice. The forces of darkness shall find no refuge within these walls while I am on the case."

With that solemn vow, David turned to address the now assembled household, his voice ringing out with authority as he addressed them. "Let it be known that I, David Walker, have been appointed by Lord Harrington to serve as his witchfinder, I will protect this household from the scourge of witchcraft. Any who seek to consort with the forces of darkness shall be brought to justice, their crimes exposed for all to see."

As David spoke, a ripple of unease passed through the gathered servants, their eyes darting nervously from one to another as they exchanged worried glances. Rose held her breath and tried to still the beating of her heart, whilst in the background Jane smirked and found herself fascinated by this powerful attractive man who spoke.

Chapter Seven
2023

Jess knocked on the door of Manor House with some trepidation. She was hoping that her cheese and onion pie would go some way to apologize for her rudeness. Edward opened the door and although he looked slightly surprised, he smiled and ushered her inside.

Jess settled into the comfortable sitting room, a faint sense of apprehension lingering as she passed the pie over to Edward, hoping to mend the rift between them.

"Edward, I brought this pie as an apology" Jess began, her voice tinged with sincerity. "I hope we can move past the misunderstanding from the other day, I know I was rude, and I can only apologize, and I would like to try and explain."

Edward nodded, a soft smile gracing his features. "Thank you, Jess, your gesture is appreciated, and I realized something was going on which would explain your haste to get rid of me" he was laughing as he said this.

Jess hesitated briefly before deciding to confide in Edward about her inexplicable experiences. "There's something I've been grappling with, a series of visions, almost like I'm seeing glimpses of another time."

Edward listened intently as Jess recounted her visions, the vivid scenes that transported her to different eras within Elders Rest. She spoke of her inability to rationalize the experiences and the haunting resonance of the visions.

"It's ever since I found the old recipe book. It's almost as if the book holds the key to these visions like the book is trying to tell me something.

Edward mulled over Jess's words, a thoughtful expression crossing his face. "The past often reveals itself in enigmatic ways. Perhaps this book holds more than just recipes?"

Jess thought for a moment, "That's what the clock mender Philip was saying, and he wanted to keep the book? Do you think I should try and speak to him again?"

"Possibly, but not alone. I also think, if you agree, that maybe I could be with you next time you read a recipe, do you think I would see visions too?"

Jess looked away. Was she ready to share these visions? She would like to spend more time with Edward and maybe it would be safer if someone was there.

"Ok I think I would be willing to try, if you don't mind," Jess said. "First let's heat that pie and we'll think about it all."

Whilst they enjoyed the pie, Edward told her more about himself and his job and his enthusiasm for local history and photography. He had been working at a school in Colne but applied for the job as head of History at Clitheroe Royal Grammar School and was really enjoying it. His photography was just a hobby but being in Harrop Fold had proved very fruitful because of all the wildlife and the beautiful scenery. Jess told him all about Grace and their bistro and how much she wanted to open another café or bistro in this area and possibly concentrate on old Lancashire recipes and pies. They enjoyed a very pleasant afternoon, and Jess was feeling very comfortable in Edward's company and hoped that he felt the same.

They eventually went back over to Elder's Rest and Jess showed Edward the old recipe book. He turned it over in his hands, not daring to open it at that stage. "Look, a bit is missing here like it's been torn off. Also, there are a lot of symbols and scripts that I have never seen before" Edward was quite mesmerized by the book. He returned the book to Jess, and she opened it randomly to a recipe for Tharf Cake **(+)**

As they both began to read the recipe, the air within the cottage once again grew cold. Jess turned to Edward. "Can you feel that?" she asked but as she was saying the words, Edward began to fade from her vision, and she could see Agnes standing by the fire…

Agnes was bathed in the soft glow of the fire, and she moved with quiet grace, her weathered hands tending to the hearth. The scent of dried herbs lingered in the air as Agnes prepared remedies, the very essence of her healing touch embedded in the atmosphere when the tranquility shattered as the door swung open with a creak. A cold draft swept through the room, extinguishing the candles in its wake. An ominous figure stood on the threshold, his eyes ablaze with a fervor that mirrored the hysteria of the times. "Agnes Thornton" his voice echoed like a dark incantation, the accusatory tone sending shivers through the room.
Agnes turned, her eyes reflecting a mix of resilience and sorrow. "What brings you here, I've done no wrong."

The man in black advanced with an air of malevolence, a parchment in hand bearing accusations that would ignite the flames of persecution. The room seemed to shrink with every step, the walls closing in on Agnes.

"I am David, the witchfinder employed by Lord Harrington. Listen very carefully Agnes for you have done his wife untold harm, you and your daughter Rose." I have been watching you and Rose. Your daughter has the mark of the devil in her eyes. The scriptures warn us of such abnormalities. 'Beware false prophets,' they say. Her eyes are but a disguise for the demon lurking within."

The witchfinder moved forward. "By the authority vested in me, you are accused of witchcraft and consorting with the devil." He declared.

Jess was finding it hard to breathe, she was shaking, and her head was pounding. She wanted to reach out and scream. "Stop leave her alone, don't take her", she was saying to herself. Suddenly the atmosphere changed, and Edward was shaking her. "Jess, Jess what is it? Stop who?"

She gazed at Edward and then around the cottage. "It happened again; they came for her" she muttered still dazed and confused.

"I saw nothing," said Edward "Obviously this book has something connecting you to the cottage and whatever happened here many years ago. Your eyes seemed focused on something that I couldn't see. I tried to talk to you, but it was as if you couldn't hear, or you weren't here. It was only when your breathing changed and you began shouting "Stop, don't take her" that I touched your shoulder and you seemed to come back."

"I think we need to talk to Philip again and also look into the history of this cottage and maybe even my grandmother." Jess 's breathing had returned to normal. "I think this book is trying to tell me something. Agnes was never tried as far as I remember Frank telling me. She disappeared apparently and was never found" Her lips began to tremble slightly.

"Ok, let's leave the book for a while and go to the library in Clitheroe and see what we can find out" Edward reassured her.

They both jumped as the front door to Elder's Rest began to slowly open, seemingly of its own accord. As they both held their breath, Bella sauntered in, giving them a very desultory stare as she made her way to the kitchen for food. The atmosphere suddenly lit up, and laughing they gathered their things together to head out to the local library.

Having finished her food, Bella made her way back into the living room and sat on top of the recipe book, purring and washing herself contentedly. She fell into a deep sleep, leaving one eye open.

Chapter Eight
1612

Harrington Hall stood silent, its opulence echoing through the corridors like a distant melody.

Agnes, wrapped in the simplicity of her worn gown, moved with a quiet purpose, carrying the potion that held the promise of hope.

As she approached Lady Evelyn Harrington's chambers, shadows seemed to dance along the ornate walls, concealing secrets within the grandeur. Unbeknownst to Agnes, a pair of eyes lingered in the dim recesses, a man recently hired by Lord Harrington, discreetly moving about the hall, but an observer to the clandestine meeting. Agnes tapped gently on the door, the rhythmic sound echoing through the hall. Rose answered, casting a quick furtive glance down the corridor before ushering Agnes inside.

Lady Harrington, adorned in silks and pearls, waited by the window with a mix of anticipation and vulnerability. The soft daylight bathed her in a warm glow, a stark contrast to the shadows that clung to the corners of the room.

"Agnes, you've come" Lady Harrington greeted, her voice a fragile melody. "Can your potions truly help me conceive?" Agnes nodded, her gaze meeting Lady Harrington's with an unspoken understanding. Rose observed the exchange, caught in the delicate dance of secrecy.

"I've brewed a concoction" Agnes explained, producing a small vial, which seemed to catch the light in a subtle otherworldly gleam. "It carries the essence of nature's blessings. Though it may not guarantee success, it holds the spirit of hope and healing."

As Lady Harrington accepted the vial, a silent pact unfolded, the promise of a shared secret, hidden from prying eyes. Agnes and Rose shared a glance, knowing the danger they could be in and the delicate balance between the desires of Lady Harrington and the expectations of the society that surrounded them. Agnes left the chamber, the soft click of the door echoing in the corridor.

In the dimness, the witchfinder lingered, his pale grey eyes cold and unblinking, a keeper of secrets bound by the unspoken code of those who tread between the light and the shadows.

However, he wasn't the only one to observe this exchange. Jane had been asked to take tea to Lady Harrington and had seen Agnes entering the bed chamber. She had listened at the door and then hidden behind a pillar as Agnes left. Jane herself was well versed in the properties of herbs as she had been taught by her grandmother. Knowing full well what the potion was that Agnes had given Lady Harrington and the hopes it held for her, she wanted not only Agnes to be in trouble but her hatred for the wealthy Harringtons was so strong that she cared little about what would happen if she were to interfere with that potion. However, she would watch and wait until the time was right and, in the meantime, she would work quietly in the kitchen, keeping her malicious thoughts to herself.

***

The atmosphere within the library was tense, as Lord Ashton Harrington a man of stern countenance, received the newly appointed Witchfinder once again. He was a figure cast in the shadows of fear and superstition that gripped 17th-century society. In the dimly lit room, Lord Harrington surveyed the man before him. David Walker was the embodiment of the burgeoning paranoia surrounding witchcraft. David, clad in dark coarse fabrics exuded an air of solemn authority. His eyes, sharp as flint and pale grey, bore the weight of zealous conviction fueled by the fervour to root out perceived darkness within the villages.

David's formative years were etched in the harsh contours of poverty and familial discord. Born into a humble cottage on the outskirts of Gisburn, he had faced a childhood marred by adversity and the unrelenting hand of a stern and uncompromising father, James Walker.

James Walker ruled the household with an iron fist and the family endured relentless financial struggles. They had meager meals, threadbare clothing, and a lack of any real warmth, physically and emotionally during the unforgiving Lancashire winters. David grew up acutely aware of the deprivation that marked his world.

Opportunities for education were a rare luxury for David. Denied the chance to expand his horizons, he grew up with a simmering frustration, perceiving education as a privilege reserved for those born into wealthier families. The family faced repeated bouts of illness and loss and this childhood laid the foundation for a resentful and embittered soul. The oppressive environment, strict paternal authority and constant struggles planted the seeds of a ruthless ambition that would later manifest in his relentless pursuit of power.

As a cunning manipulator, David discovered the power he could wield by exploiting the fear and suspicions of the community. He realized that branding individuals as witches granted him influence and authority. He had a deep-rooted resentment of women due to his mother being too weak and afraid to stand up to his father James and simply watched when David was given a vicious beating.

Over time, David developed a callous indifference to the suffering of others. His heart hardened against empathy, allowing him to execute his ruthless agenda without remorse. David Walker's transformation into a malevolent witchfinder was a culmination of personal traumas, societal pressures, and a thirst for control. In a world teeming with uncertainty, he found solace in the perverse authority granted to those who wielded accusations of witchcraft.

Lord Harrington, a man of austere bearing, regarded the Witchfinder with a mixture of skepticism and compliance. The very notion of witchcraft had become a festering sore in the collective consciousness of the time, stoked by tales of the devilry and the supernatural.

"Mr Walker, I've appointed you to ensure the purity of this estate. Witchcraft is a stain that must be eradicated, "Lord Harrington declared, his words laden with the weight of social expectations and pressures. David's eyes gleamed with fervent zeal as he responded, "My Lord, as I have said, I shall leave no stone unturned. The Devil's minions must be rooted out and purged from these lands. I must protect this estate from the clutches of the infernal."

"Is there anything to report here, at Harrington Hall "queried Lord Harrington.

David hesitated, his pale grey eyes giving nothing away. He would keep what he saw to himself until he had investigated further. The fact that Lady Harrington may be involved somehow would take some careful thought and handling. "Nothing untoward here my Lord," he replied with a smile.

As the Witchfinder took his leave, the darkened corridors seemed to absorb the echoes of his solemn pronouncements. The fear of witchcraft hung in the air, a palpable presence that permeated every nook and cranny of Harrington Hall.

David Walker, a man forged in the crucible of devoutness and piety, had become the harbinger of suspicion. His arrival signaled an era where shadows whispered of dark deeds, and the accused found themselves at the mercy of an inquisition fueled by the relentless pursuit of the supernatural.

In the tapestry of fear and uncertainty, Lord Harrington and his newly appointed Witchfinder stood poised to confront the imagined threats that lurked in the obscured corners of their world. The lines between the accused and the accusers blurred, setting the stage for a drama where justice and innocence danced on the precipice of the unknown.

Chapter Nine
2023

Edward and Jess made their way into the old market town of Clitheroe. Edward had recently bought an old Jimny Jeep anticipating that he would need a four-by-four for these roads when winter came. He had bought the car from a friend of Frank's. George owned Ribble Cars in Clitheroe and specialized in second-hand cars and Edward was pleased with the car and the price and enjoyed driving it. From Elders Rest and the hamlet of Harrop Fold, the lane wound down to the main road. It was a single track and tricky if another car was coming the opposite way. He was also learning to look out for pheasants and hares who would cross the lane from the fields, especially in the early morning when he was driving to work. Just past the Chapel, there was a small caravan park that Frank also ran. There was one tent and a camper van parked on it. As they passed by Jess could see a man wearing a hat, hanging out his washing. As they slowed down to allow a tractor to go past, Jess realized that the man was naked!

"Edward, look. Am I imagining things or is that man hanging his washing out naked?"

Edward looked over and laughed "Yes, I think he is "and with that started to wave at him. The naked man smiled and waved back, as if it was the most natural thing in the world.

"Oh my god "laughed Jess "Wait till I tell Frank.". They were still laughing as they reached the end of the lane.

That day the scenery was stunning. As they made their way over the tops the view of the valley was outstanding with the ever-present view of Pendle and the villages below. They had to slow down for two horses on their way past Broomhill where there was a Riding School and then dropped down into the village of Grindleton with its long winding road down towards Clitheroe. Passing over the river they saw a Heron on the banks, the fields covered in a low mist.

The town had retained much of its old character and customs and had a wide range of shops, many of which had been run by the same family for generations. A popular open-air market was held on Tuesdays, Thursdays, and Saturdays. The main street of the town was dominated by a massive rock of limestone crowned with the Keep of an ancient castle. The Castle grounds contained formal gardens, tennis courts, bowling green, and a cafeteria. There was a large open-air auditorium with a bandstand where concerts ranging from brass bands to rock music could be heard in the summer.

The library which was established in 1905 was situated at a fork of two roads. The narrowest part of the building featured a turret with a clock and a conical roof.

On entering they made enquiries and found themselves upstairs in the old records department. There was a lot to go through so they each sat at a different table and started to meticulously search through all the old documents the library had provided.

As Edward immersed himself in the faded records, a particular parchment drew his discerning eye. It chronicled the haunting tale of Elders Rest and the hamlet of Harrop Fold during the 17th Century, especially the disappearance of Agnes Thornton, a healer whose cottage stood as a silent witness to the accusations that tainted the village. The inked words spoke of whispered conspiracies and the vanishing act that cast a pall over the name of Elders Rest.

Meanwhile, Jess, guided by an intuition that seemed to echo through time, discovered an old journal that chronicled the harrowing fate of Agnes's daughter, Rose. The yellowed pages whispered of accusations unjustly hurled, of a daughter's anguish, the ominous shadows that clung to Elders Rest like a curse. It narrated the tale of Rose, accused of witchcraft in the aftermath of her mother's mysterious disappearance. The legend spoke of a relentless pursuit by the Witchfinder, a man named David, who sought to cleanse the village of perceived darkness.

As the revelation unfolded, Jess realized that her life was intricately woven into the tapestry of Elders Rest and that through the old recipe book, the legend of Agnes and Rose was not just a distant tale but a living history that resonated with the whispers of the present.

They borrowed the documents that were of interest and returned to Harrop Fold. As they sat in the living room, the stillness enveloped Edward and Jess as they pored over the aged documents that chronicled the village's history. The grandfather clock, an ever-present witness, ticked softly in the background.

Edward looked up from a stack of old letters, his eyes meeting Jess's gaze. "There's a remarkable consistency between your visions and these historical accounts," he remarked, his tone a blend of fascination and validation. Jess nodded, her fingers tracing the notes they'd compiled. "It's as if the recipe book is a bridge between the past and present, guiding me through these echoes of time."

Edward's eyes shifted to the open recipe book on the table. "Perhaps it holds the key to unraveling the mysteries of this cottage and whatever befell poor Agnes and Rose. What if we use it as a guide? Go through each recipe and see what unfolds. A hesitant excitement crept into Jess's voice. "You mean, follow the recipes as a narrative, letting them reveal the story?"
Edward smiled, "Exactly. Your visions have provided glimpses, but this book might offer a more detailed account. You could uncover the secrets that time has concealed."

Jess's eyes brightened with a newfound determination. "Let's do it, Edward. Let's dive into the book, piece by piece, and see where the recipes lead us."

Edward smiled at Jess, feeling the same excitement but he was also worried. "Ok, but you must promise me to do this together. I don't think it's safe for you to have these visions when you're on your own Jess."

"Deal, but that might mean you have to spend quite some time here with me" Jess chuckled looking at Edward. "I'm sure I can manage that", he responded with a smile that lit up his whole face, and for the first time in the last year, Jess began to feel something resembling hope and a sense of peace coming back to her.

Edward picked up the old book from the bookcase where Jess had stored it. "Well, there's no time like the present", he said enthusiastically. Jess took the book off him "Let's start at the beginning, if I remember from my brief peruse of the book it was a recipe for Hindle Wakes * which involves a chicken, which I don't have so I may have to go shopping."

Together they opened the old parchment pages. There was the recipe for Hindle Wakes which was quite difficult to read and there were many symbols and scribblings alongside. They both glanced at each other as if waiting for something to happen. Jess quickly wrote the ingredients down, still glancing around the cottage as if it was suddenly going to disappear. "Okay, I'll go shopping, and then later, if you want to come over, we can begin?" Jess suggested. Edward agreed and as he left, he took the old documents that they had retrieved from the library. "I'll have another read through all these, I think, see what else I can discover.".

They went their separate ways, both excited and a little nervous as to what was going to happen on their journey of discovery. As Jess was leaving the cottage, she felt as if she was being watched. She glanced around the room but there was nothing and nobody there. As she got to her car, she looked up and saw a glimpse of red hair disappear behind the old barn. Who was this girl that she kept seeing? She set off for the shops determined to discuss this with Edward and maybe Frank when she next saw him.

Later that evening over a glass of red wine, they began the first part of the recipe which involved soaking some prunes overnight in lemon juice. Nothing untoward happened and although a bit disappointed, Jess was in some ways also relieved. Maybe the old book wasn't the means of discovering what happened. However, she also remembered what the clock mender Philip said. **"Whisper of powers long slumbering, of a heritage entwined with Lancashire's**

darkest folklore, not just recipes as it would appear."

She decided then and there not to tell Edward, but she would contact Philip again and see if he could clarify his strange words. They had a very pleasant evening and agreed to meet up later the next day to finish the recipe.

After Edward had left the cottage, Jess fed Bella and began to get herself ready for bed.

As she picked up the recipe book to put in the kitchen for tomorrow, she glanced again at the first recipe for Hindle Wakes. The atmosphere within Elders Rest changed suddenly, she could feel the heat of a fire, even though her wood burner still wasn't working. She glanced around and gasped, her shock making her stumble back onto the settee.

The flames in the hearth cast a warm glow on the aged stones of Elders Rest. Agnes, with the air of a guardian of ancient secrets, moved gracefully around the room adorned with dried herbs and potions. Rose, perched on a worn wooden stool, gazed into the flickering fire, her expression a mix of contemplation and worry.

The flames flickered, casting dancing shadows on the walls of Elders Rest. In the quiet hum of the cottage, the dialogue between past and present unfolded, dialogue etched in the very stones that bore witness to the struggles of healers and the dangers of misunderstood magic.

"Do you think your potion will help Lady Harrington, mother?" Rose said softly.

"The potion Rose is a concoction born from nature's embrace and the artistry of the craft. It bears the weight of hope and the delicate dance of life" Agnes smiled.

"But what if," Rose said, tracing patterns on her stool, "What if the potion's magic brings not only life but also the suspicions of those who fear what they do not understand?"

Agnes leaned in, her eyes meeting Rose's. "Our craft, Rose, is as much about protecting as it is about healing. These times are fraught with shadows, and the wind carries whispers that could ignite the flames of fear. Rose gazed around the cottage, with its low ceiling and crooked beams, it seemed to hold within its very structure the memories of countless moments shared between mother and daughter. Her gaze went to the vials on the shelves. The wind whispers of witchfinders and dark times.

Elders Rest feels like a sanctuary she thought, but could it become a prison in these times? She expressed her thoughts to Agnes.

Agnes nodded "Elders Rest, our haven, must be shielded from the storm. Our craft, our legacy, is a secret that time has entrusted to us. We must tread cautiously, for the eyes of suspicion are sharp." Rose got up and began pacing the room. "You know Lord Harrington has hired a witchfinder, he addressed the servants this morning and is determined to seek out witchcraft within our villages. I have seen him looking at me as if he already knows something "Rose looked worried.

Agnes gave a short laugh "Witchfinders are like Wolves Rose, sniffing for scent where there is none. Let's have no more of this talk, we have Hindle Wakes to make my love."

The room became cold again and Jess found herself sitting on the settee with the old recipe book at her side. She shook her head, trying to make sense. It was as if they had been with her in this very room. It was the first time she had heard Rose, and she realized with shock that this was the girl that she kept seeing. She already knew that Agnes and Rose were mother and daughter and lived at Elders Rest. She knew that Agnes disappeared and that Rose was later accused of witchcraft, but what was the connection?

She knew now that Agnes had given Lady Harrington some sort of potion, for what purposes Jess wasn't sure. She felt a headache coming on and decided to go up to bed. As she tried to sleep her mind kept going over her visions. Someone was coming for Agnes and had accused her of being a witch. Agnes had made some sort of potion to give to Lady Harrington, but what was she missing, what happened next? She tossed and turned and finally fell into a fitful sleep wondering where the comforting presence of Bella was.

Bella didn't come up with her that night, she settled herself in front of the cold fire, mewing slightly then curling up to sleep, with one eye open as she rested.

Chapter Ten
1612
Two Months Later

It was a cold day when David emerged from Harrington Hall to walk around the surrounding villages on his daily rounds. He cut a figure that seemed to emerge from the very shadows he chased. Tall and lean, his silhouette carried an air of both authority and menace, like a raven poised to take flight from a darkened perch. His cloak, a deep shade of midnight, billowed around him, seemingly woven from the fabric of the shadows he traversed. His eyes, sharp as flint, bore into the heart of the village, piercing the veil of everyday life with an intensity that seemed to strip away pretenses. It was said his gaze alone could unravel the secrets that were hidden within the humble cottages and winding lanes.

A mane of jet-black hair cascaded down his shoulders, framing a face that seemed untouched by the passage of time. His features, chiseled and unyielding, carried an unsettling charisma that drew both fear and fascination from those who crossed his path. David moved with an eerie grace, casting an aura of authority that lent weight to his every step. Villagers couldn't help averting their gaze when he passed, as if his cloak held the power to ensnare wandering souls. As he traversed the villages, his presence left an indelible mark, a shadow that clung to the timeworn walls and whispered tales of suspicion and accusation.

He had news from Harrington Hall and his suspicions were aroused. He was making his way to Elders Rest to confront the wise woman Agnes before he took his theories to Lord Harrington.

***

Within Harrington Hall, the seasons had begun to change, and with them, the whispers of hope had started to unfurl. Lady Harrington moved through the corridors with a certain hesitancy, her steps measured as if the weight of the past still clung to her every movement. The morning sunbathed Lady Harrington's chambers in a soft, golden glow. She stood before the mirror, her hand resting gently on her abdomen. Unspoken prayers hung in the air as she held her breath, awaiting a revelation that might change the course of Harrington Hall's fate. Lady Harrington's eyes widened as the realization dawned. She traced the contours of her stomach, a tender smile playing on her lips. The joy that had eluded the hall for so long seemed to find a foothold in her heart. In the quietude of her chamber, Lady Harrington reveled in the secret she held. A seed of new life that promised to bloom in the wake of tragedy. The promise of an heir, a fragile flame rekindled against the backdrop of lingering shadows.

Meanwhile, in the shadows of Elders Rest, Agnes went about her routine, unaware of the stirrings of fate. David, with eyes sharp as obsidian, strode purposefully toward Elders Rest. His cloak billowed in the wind like a dark omen as he approached Agnes, who was tending to some herbs near the cottage door.

David hid himself in the shadows. He watched silently as Agnes gathered her herbs and returned inside. With a cunning that only he had, he managed to position himself so that he could see everything going on without being observed by Agnes. He saw her mixing herbs, filling vials, and muttering. His steely gaze watched as Agnes went over to the bookcase which was situated next to the big fireplace. She touched a book named Precartio Omnium Herbarum, and as the bookcase swung open, he could see that there was a cleverly concealed room behind it. His steely gaze observed Agnes as she began to store her vials away and then closed the bookcase, making sure the book she had touched was back in place. He grinned to himself and stored this information within his cunning mind. He was a highly intelligent man and knew well what the book was. It was a prayer to herbs.

"Man, I prescribe ye may have favourable issues and most speedy result. That I may ever be allowed, with the favour of your majesty, to gather you...and I shall set forth the produce of the fields for you to return thanks through the name of the mother who ordained your birth."

As she came back outside, he appeared out of nowhere, startling her.

"Agnes, he sneered, his voice cutting through the calm, "I know of your visits to Lady Harrington. What concoctions have you made, and what may you have taken to her?"

Agnes turned to face him, her gaze unwavering. "I bring no harm, only remedies for a heart heavy with grief. The herbs I carry are not spells but salves to soothe wounds unseen."

David's eyes narrowed; suspicion etched across his features. "I will be watching,

Agnes. The shadows may hide your secrets for now, but darkness has a way of revealing even the most well-guarded truths." "I suggest you tread very carefully as I will not rest if I suspect any witchcraft is afoot. I will be watching your daughter Rose too as she goes about her work at the Hall." With that he swept off down the path, giving a small black cat a swift kick on his way.

***

In Harrington Hall, the kitchen bustled with activity as the midday meal preparations were underway. Peggy Higgins, the cook, moved hurriedly among the pots and pans, her hands trembling as she attempted to keep pace with the demands of the kitchen. Suddenly, her movements grew erratic, her eyes widening in terror as she clutched at her chest. A strangled gasp escaped her lips, and she collapsed to the floor in a convulsive fit. The other servants recoiled in horror, unsure of what to do as the cook thrashed and writhed on the ground.

Amidst the chaos, David, the witchfinder on his return from Elders Rest, arrived on the scene, drawn by the commotion. Rose, who was also in the kitchen at that time, looked on in horror at David, as his eyes gleamed with sinister excitement as he observed Peggy's distress. With a flourish, he declared "Behold, the devil's handiwork at play! This maid has been bewitched, no doubt". He glanced around and his eyes locked on Rose, and he grinned menacingly.

Lord Harrington, having been alerted to the disturbance, strode into the kitchen, his brow furrowed with concern. "What is the meaning of this?" he demanded, his voice booming with authority. As he was rarely seen below the stairs, the rest of the servants were quiet and shocked by this turn of events.

David stepped forward, his voice dripping with conviction. "My lord, this poor soul has fallen victim to the dark arts. Only the water's judgment can reveal the truth of her innocence or guilt. We must subject her to the swimming test at once!" Jane, who had been observing the events in the background of the kitchen, smiled to herself. She had no fondness for the cook and was looking forward to what might happen next. "No", shouted Rose, "surely, she is just unwell "She looked at Lord Harrington pleadingly. Lord Harrington hesitated, torn between his duty to his servants and his fear of witchcraft.

"Well, witchfinder, shall we call for the physician?" he demanded. Jane suddenly spoke "No my lord I fear the witchfinder is right I have seen Peggy consorting with others in the village and believe she may even be part of a secret coven "she lied.

"That's not true, "said Rose with disbelief, please let us help her, before condemning her." David looked straight at Rose as he said, "No, it is obvious that she has been possessed by the devil and we must do the witch test immediately. If she is innocent, it will be revealed."

"Very well, if it must be done, then let it be done," Lord Harrington suddenly announced to the other servants' horror. Jane merely smirked in the background as she glanced at Rose.

Rose looked on in despair as Peggy was lifted from the floor and carried out into the gardens of the hall and down to the large lake within the grounds. She was stripped naked and tied with a rope. David made sure that it was done correctly, and her right thumb was tied to her left big toe. She was then thrust into a sack and with David controlling the rope, she was dunked into the water three times.

Rose looked on in horror as each time she bobbed back up to the surface. She knew in her heart that David was controlling the rope, but she was powerless to do anything. David, his eyes ablaze with triumph, proclaimed

"See how the waters have spared her! This is the work of the devil, but fear not, for we shall root out his minions wherever they may hide! She should be burnt at the stake immediately. He glanced over at Rose once again. Lord Harrington nodded, his expression grave.

"I fear what you say is true, witchfinder" he replied and although doubt gnawed at his heart, he agreed with his witchfinder, "Take her away and burn her and make the servants watch so they may be reminded of the consequences of consorting with the devil." He strode back into the Hall without a backward glance.

To the horror and distress of the gathered servants, they watched as poor Peggy was taken to a hastily constructed wooden pyre and bound to the stake with rope. The cook, her once vibrant demeanor now subdued by fear, stood, her hands clasped tightly in prayer, her eyes wide with terror. The servants murmured amongst themselves as the executioner approached. With practiced efficiency, he ignited the kindling at the base of the pyre, sending tendrils of smoke spiraling upwards into the ashen sky. As the fire began to consume the dry timber, the cook's agonized screams pierced the air, echoing around the grounds. The acrid scent of burning flesh mingled with the smoke, assaulting the senses of those gathered to witness the grim spectacle.

David, his watchful eyes still on Rose, led the crowd in chants of condemnation, his voice rising above the crackle of the fire.

Rose watched in silence her heart heavy. In the flickering light of the inferno, the shadow of suspicion stretched long and dark, casting a pall of fear and uncertainty over all who bore witness to the witch's trial.

Chapter Eleven
2023

Jess looked at Edward, her eyes reflecting the weight of the visions that haunted her. She took a deep breath, hesitated for a moment then began to tell him of her latest journey through time.

"I saw them," Jess began, her voice a melodic whisper. "Agnes and Rose, here in Elders Rest. Shadows clung to the walls, but the flickering candlelight revealed their figures. They spoke in hushed tones, their hands moving with a familiarity that spoke of shared secrets."

Edward, captivated by Jess's words, leaned forward. "What were they discussing?"

"A potion," Jess continued. "A concoction that Agnes held in a vial, a mixture of herbs and whispered incantations. They spoke of a Lady Harrington, her grief, and the promise of a remedy that could bring solace to her heart."

As Jess recounted the scene, a gust of wind blew open the recipe book that had been sitting beside them as if responding to words that Jess had just recounted. They both jumped and stared at each other in horror. Edward's mind raced, connecting the dots between the visions and the enigmatic book of recipes and symbols. Edward, his eyes scanning the symbols with the meticulous gaze of a historian, noted their intricate design. "These symbols", he remarked, "are not mere recipes. They seem to be a language, a guide maybe that Agnes and Rose left for those who possess the key to understanding.

Jess nodded, her connection to the symbols and recipes growing with each revelation. "It's as if the book is a vessel of alchemy, a history maybe of events that occurred here?"

They immersed themselves in the pages once again and the room pulsed with an energy that bridged the tangible and the ethereal.

"There's a Harrington Hall in Downham, do you think that is one connection" remarked Jess suddenly.

"Quite likely. Why don't we finish that recipe off for Hindle Wakes and see if we can gather any more information, or at least see if you can, but I am staying with you." Edward put an arm around Jess and pulled her close.

As they made the chicken recipe and enjoyed it immensely, giving Bella some too, they settled on the settee to discuss further recipes and the investigation of Harrington Hall.

***

As she took a sip of her wine, the cottage became cold and her vision was hazy. Jess could smell lavender and the living room of Elders Rest was slowly fading. She realized that she was seeing a bedroom where the centerpiece of the room was a grand canopy bed, draped with heavy brocade curtains in vibrant hues of deep burgundy and gold, that cascaded like waterfalls. The living room at Elders Rest began to fade even more until all she could see was a very elegant lady gazing into an ornate mirror.

Gilded frames adorned the walls, housing portraits of ancestors and those who had graced the halls of Harrington Hall in times past. Their eyes seemed to watch over the room, witnesses to the events that were unfolding. The furnishings were exquisite. A silken chaise lounge rested near the window; its fabric kissed by the soft glow of sunlight that filtered through heavy drapes. A crystal chandelier hung from the ceiling, casting a gentle illumination that refracted off tear-shaped crystals. Large bouquets of flowers adorned tables and dressers and the whole room smelt of lavender and roses.

A mahogany writing desk stood in a corner, its surface cluttered with parchment and quills, and the room was meticulously maintained.

A grand mirror stood against one wall, its reflection capturing the image of a woman adorned in an ensemble that blended sophistication and contemporary grace. Lady Harrington stood in front of the mirror with an aura of refined elegance, her posture regal and graceful, and she radiated an understated dignity that would surely capture the attention of onlookers. She wore a full-length dress, tastefully adorned with subtle patterns. The fabric, with a gentle sway, moved with each step. The colour palette of her attire was harmonized earthy tones, blending soft greys, with hints of moss green. These subdued hues complemented her complexion, casting a soft and inviting glow that revealed a woman at ease with her own sense of style. Her hair was elegantly coiffed, and a pair of pearl earrings dangled gently, catching the light in delicate reflections. A simple bracelet graced her wrist. As Jess gazed at her reflection in the mirror, she could see that Lady Harrington's eyes were a warm and inviting deep brown that held a depth that seemed to invite connection.

Lady Harrington was gently stoking the contours of her stomach and was smiling to herself.
She turned from the mirror, looked directly at Jess, and smiled.

Jess jumped off the settee and looked around her. "I'm here." Said Edward gently as he softly pulled Jess back down. "So, it would appear it is only you who is going to get the visions. Are you ok? What did you see?"
Jess looked at Edward. "She's pregnant…Lady Harrington, I saw her. Agnes's potion has worked" ……………

***

Later that evening after Edward had left, Jess was standing at the window gazing over the hamlet and out to the fells in the distance, she saw Bella in the fields hunting something, she was very adept at catching mice and birds and would disappear for hours at a time. As she turned away smiling, her eye caught something near the back gate. Just for a fleeting second, she saw the girl, with long red hair, dressed in a long brown tunic, gazing intently at Elders Rest. She gasped, "Rose?" As she continued to look the vision of the girl faded in the mist and all she could see again were the fields and fells in the distance. Jess remembered the visions where someone was coming after Agnes. Could it be something to do with Lady Harrington and her pregnancy? There was something sinister and it was worrying her. Jess shivered. What was happening? She should be frightened, but instead, a steely determination began to seep into her very soul, and she vowed to herself that she would find out the truth one way or another.

The following day Edward and Jess set off for the village of Downham to investigate Harrington Hall. There was a tour that afternoon, so they decided to go to the local pub, The Assheton Arms, and have some lunch. The pub had been closed due to the pandemic and had recently been taken over by a local hotelier who had other pubs and restaurants in the area. The pub was in a lovely setting within the village, with stunning views of Pendle Hill. It had flagstone floors, low ceilings, and ancient timbers. It was oozing with history, character and charm.

As they took a seat and perused the menu, Edward took hold of Jess's hand.

"I'm so glad we met and that we can investigate this together Jess" he smiled at her.

"Me too, and thank you", Jess looked into his eyes and felt a warmth enveloping her. As they continued to chat over some drinks, Jess decided to have the Lamb Shank Pie mainly because it was something she herself had never made. It came with hotpot potatoes and sticky red cabbage and Edward chose the Cowmans sausage and mash. Cowmans sausage shop was famous in Clitheroe. It had been a butcher for over 120 years and even had its own abattoir at the rear which had closed in the early 1970's. They produced quality sausages sourced from local auctions and the pigs they used were outdoor reared. Their food arrived and it was delicious. Jess told Edward all about her friends Adeline, Melissa and Jeanette, and Edward shared stories of his childhood and university days. They finished and paid and made their way over to the Hall for the tour.

Harrington Hall stood as a grand testament to centuries of history and aristocratic opulence. Its imposing façade loomed over meticulously landscaped grounds, surrounded by lush Gardens and ancient trees. The Hall was situated in a serene corner of the village of Downham, its presence both commanding and elegant.

The exterior of the Hall had tall leaded windows and chimneys punctuating the brick façade. Ivy gracefully climbed the stone walls, giving the mansion an air of enduring beauty. The main entrance was flanked by colossal oak doors adorned with elaborate ironwork. The expansive gardens surrounding the hall featured manicured lawns, vibrant flowerbeds and a labyrinthine maze that whispered of aristocratic leisure. A carriage drive swept around a central fountain, while a serpentine path led to a kitchen garden, still alive with fresh herbs.

As Edward and Jess entered the Hall, they were greeted by a grand foyer adorned with a sweeping staircase, its banister carved with intricate patterns. The floors were polished to a shine, reflecting the soft glow of the crystal chandeliers overhead. The walls were adorned with ancestral portraits, capturing the stern faces of the Harringtons from generations past. They both gazed at the portrait of Lord Ashton Harrington and Lady Evelyn Harrington, both acknowledging the confirmation they had sought. The drawing room was a lavish space, with plush velvet drapes framing tall windows that overlooked the estate. Antique furniture upholstered in rich fabrics sat on oriental rugs that added a touch of exoticism. A grand piano occupied one corner, a silent witness to the musical soirees that once graced these hallowed halls.

The library was a treasure trove of leather-bound volumes, housing the collected knowledge of generations. A large fireplace provided warmth; its mantle was adorned with ancestral crests. The scent of aged parchment and polished wood permeated the air.

Upstairs the bed chambers were opulent retreats, draped in sumptuous fabrics and featuring four poster beds with intricately carved headboards. Each room was adorned with family heirlooms and relics, creating a real sense of continuity and tradition that permeated the hall.

Jess was in one of the bedrooms whilst Edward had moved on to another room when she looked in one of the mirrors. She gasped as she caught a fleeting reflection of Rose. However, the ghostly image was accompanied by a sense of warmth and familiarity. Rose's eyes met Jess's in the reflection as if trying to convey a message to her. Just as swiftly as it came, the image disappeared.

***

Later that day Jess called Adeline and Melissa and agreed to meet them for a drink at a local pub. Jess needed to talk things through with her friends and tell them about Edward too.

As she opened the door of the Waddington Arms, in the lovely village of Waddington the soft glow of dimmed lights cast a warm ambiance and the scent of oak aged wine and the crackling fire was welcoming and comforting. Jess scanned the room until she spotted Adeline and Melissa nestled in two large cozy chairs towards the back of the pub.

"Hey, there she is!" Adeline exclaimed, waving Jess over with a grin.

Jess grinned back, her steps quickening as she made her way over to them. She sat in a chair beside them, already feeling the weight of the day lift off her shoulders in their presence.

"Cheers, ladies" Melissa said, raising her glass of rich red wine. "To good friends and even better wine."

They clinked their glasses together, the sound echoing softly in the bustling pub.

"Cheers" Jess said, taking a sip of her own wine and savouring the velvety notes of blackberry and spice. As they reminisced about old times and shared stories of their latest adventures, Jess found herself opening up about Edward and the mysterious happenings at Elders Rest. Adeline and Melissa listened intently, offering words of encouragement and support.

"Sounds like you've got your hands full Jess," Adeline said, swirling her wine thoughtfully. "But hey at least you've got Edward by your side through all of it, right?"

Jess nodded, a soft smile tugging at the corners of her lips. "Yeah, he's been amazing, I don't know what I would do without him."

Melissa raised an eyebrow teasingly, "Ooh, sounds like things are getting serious "

"Not quite yet," Jess blushed, "But who knows what the future holds?" Adeline looked at Jess and leaned forward.

"Come on, spill the beans Jess, is he hot and have you, you know…." She laughed.

"Trust you to ask that" Jess laughed, "Yes he is and I'm not telling you!!"

They all laughed and Melissa ordered more wine. For a moment Jess forgot about the mysteries of Elders Rest, content to be in the company of her closest friends. As the evening stretched on, they lingered over their wine, lost in conversation and laughter. For

Jess, there was nowhere else she would rather be than surrounded by their warmth and friendship and the promise of tomorrow.

Chapter Twelve
1612

Within the opulent chambers of Harrington Hall, Lady Harrington harbored a secret that bore both hope and trepidation. Lord Ashton Harrington, a stern figure with a demeanor that mirrored the stone walls of his ancestral home, sat in a high-backed chair as Lady Harrington prepared to share news that would reshape the course of their legacy. The flickering candlelight cast shadows on the ornate tapestries lining the walls, and a fire crackled in the hearth, creating an atmosphere tinged with warmth and solemnity. Lady Harrington, adorned in a gown that draped her small burgeoning form with grace, approached her husband with a mixture of anticipation and anxiety. The moment of revelation hung in the air like a delicate veil.

"My Lord, I bear news that will bring both joy and responsibility to our household." "Speak, Lady Harrington" he said with a stern expression. "What news do you bring that warrants such ceremony? Lady Harrington said with a delicate smile "I am with child, my lord. Our legacy will endure, and Harrington Hall will echo with the laughter of a new generation."

A brief pause followed as Lord Harrington absorbed the weight of this revelation. His features softened, if only slightly, as the realization of impending fatherhood began to sink in.

"An heir. Our legacy is secure. This is welcome news, Evelyn, my love. We must celebrate my darling." He rang the bell for Winthrop and proceeded to tell him the good news. A party was planned, and all the servants were to celebrate too.

"Bring me some Wine, Winthrop, and tell all our good news. Call the physicians I wish Lady Harrington to be examined immediately to make sure all is well "Lord Harrington boomed ecstatically. As Lord and Lady Harrington toasted to their future heir, the flames of the hearth cast a warm glow on the celebrations.

However, a shadow outside the Hall's grand entrance betrayed a presence with far darker intentions. Rose was in the kitchen of the Hall when the news filtered down about Lady Harrington. Although she was pleased, it worried her too and she would have to tell

Agnes that evening if she could manage to get away to Elders Rest. Had the potion worked, she thought or was it just coincidence?

Later that day, because of all the celebrations, Rose was allowed some time off to go and see her mother. She set off to Elders Rest, unaware that she was being watched.

***

Rose, with long red locks cascading in loose waves around her shoulders, possessed an otherworldly beauty. Her eyes, which were an unusual combination, as one eye was green and one was brown, held a pearl of quiet wisdom. Clad in a simple gown, the fabric swirled around her ankles as she moved, and a modest apron adorned her slender frame. David, hidden in the shadows, observed Rose from a distance. The flickering lanterns cast a play of light and shadow on his calculating expression as he formulated a plan. The allure of forbidden knowledge and the prospect of unraveling the secrets of Elders Rest fueled his sinister intentions. He had been watching Rose for a while and found her very attractive. Together with her connections to Elders Rest, he had decided she was a very enticing prospect.

With a predatory grace, David approached Rose, his footsteps masked by the night's embrace. His attire, a cloak of darkness that seemed to meld with shadows, concealed the malevolence that lurked beneath the surface.

"Good evening, dear Rose," he murmured, his voice carrying a disarming charm that belied his ulterior motives. "Such a beauty deserves to revel in the grandeur of Harrington Hall with all the others. Would you care to accompany me back there? Where are you off to in such a hurry?"
"I'm going to see my mother and then I will return to the Hall" Rose unsuspecting and innocent replied.

"Maybe I could accompany you there and then walk you back to the hall." David was staring intently at Rose.

The air crackled with an unspoken tension, as the witchfinder extended the invitation, concealing the sinister agenda that simmered beneath the veneer of politeness. Rose didn't like David and certainly didn't want him to accompany her to Elders Rest, but she didn't want to offend him either, she didn't trust him.

"Very well I will accompany you back to the Hall and see my mother tomorrow, Sir. "Rose very reluctantly decided.

As they walked, David turned to her. "I've been meaning to get you on your own for some time Rose, I have a proposal." Rose looked up her expression guarded as she met his gaze.

"What do you want, Mr Walker?" He looked around to make sure no one else was there and that they couldn't be overheard.

"I have always admired you Rose; you are a very attractive young lady. I wondered if you would consider or shall I say allow me, to court you?"

Rose was horrified. The witchfinder, whilst being a very attractive man, also made her feel very uncomfortable and she hated the pale grey eyes that looked at her with such intent.

"I'm sorry Mr Walker, but I am already courting" was the only thing she could think of. She didn't want to offend Lord Harrington's witchfinder but she certainly didn't want his attentions either.

"Come now Rose, we both know that that's not true. I think you should consider my terms; it would be beneficial to both of us, my dear." He almost snarled as he delivered these words.

"I'm sorry Mr Walker but as I said I am already courting," Rose said almost in desperation. She was looking around the lanes hoping another servant would appear so she could make her escape.

"I think that I need to see my mother, Sir, I shall return to the hall later." As she turned to leave, the witchfinder grabbed her arm, hard. David's expression changed and he stared at Rose with undisguised disgust. He wasn't going to be rejected by the likes of a servant girl, however attractive she may be.

"I saw what your mother did,", his tone low and insistent. "I saw her take that potion, the one that brought about Lady Harrington's condition."

Rose's eyes widened slightly, a flicker of apprehension crossing her features. "I don't know what you're talking about."

"Don't play dumb with me," Rose "David said, his voice taking on a harder edge. "I know what I saw. And I suspect that you have the same abilities as your mother. If anything were to happen to Lady Harrington or her unborn child, it could point to the potion that was given to her by your mother." Rose stiffened, her hands were beginning to sweat and her heart was beating wildly. "What do you want from me?"

David stepped closer, his gaze intense. "I want you to understand the gravity of the situation. Your mother's actions could be considered treasonous. You know of Lord Harrington's fears and suspicions regarding witchcraft, Rose? After all, you were there when the unfortunate cook met her demise."

"I was Sir, "Rose's mind was whirring with this revelation. "But I have no idea what you are talking about, I know nothing about any potions."

David sneered "I think you do, but I may be willing to overlook what I saw…if you agree to my terms."

Rose regarded him warily "And what terms would those be?" she said fearfully, although in her heart she already knew what he was going to say.

David's lips curved into a sly smile. "I want you by my side. If we were to be seen together, it would dispel any rumours about your involvement in your mother's schemes. And perhaps, in time, we could come to an understanding."

Rose's jaw clenched, her gaze narrowing. "So, you're blackmailing me."

David shrugged nonchalantly. "Call it what you will. But consider this, Rose. Your mother's fate lies in your hands. I suggest you give the matter some thought. Come, we need to return to the Hall." David strode on ahead. Unbeknownst to her, Rose stood at the crossroads of celebration and impending danger, her fate intertwined with the shadows that trailed her every step. Instead of going to Elders Rest, Rose decided to accompany the witchfinder back to the hall. She didn't trust him and was worried not only for herself but also for her mother Agnes.

As Rose and David began their walk back to the Hall, a pair of feline eyes observed the unfolding drama. Elders Rest's resident cat, a sleek and mysterious creature named Belladonna, moved with a silent grace through the hamlet's narrow streets. Belladonna, a creature of the night with fur as dark as the bewitching hour, prowled the cobblestone paths with an air of silent knowing. Her eyes, a pair of gleaming emeralds that caught the ambient moonlight, hinted at a feline intelligence that transcended the ordinary.

While the revelry echoed from Harrington Hall above, Belladonna sensed the currents of danger that danced beneath the surface. Cats, known as keen observers of the supernatural, carried an ancient wisdom that often-eluded human comprehension. As David, the witchfinder, extended his invitation to Rose with a charm that concealed his real intentions, Belladonna's ears twitched. Sensing an anomaly in the atmosphere, the cat slinked closer, weaving through the shadows like a wraith. The cat approached Rose with a soft purr, brushing against her legs. Rose feeling the gentle nudge of Belladonna against her, looked down at the cat with a fond smile.

"Ah Bella" she said, bending down to stroke the cat's sleek fur. "What brings you here, my friend?

Belladonna moved away towards David, silently winding herself around his legs. At the unexpected touch against his boots, he looked down to see the dark form of the cat. Her emerald eyes gleamed knowingly, and the witchfinder's expression twisted in distaste. He recoiled slightly, his allergies triggered by the proximity of the feline presence, something that the cat was aware of. "Cursed creatures" David muttered suppressing a sneeze. His eyes narrowed, not only in response to the cat but also fueled by a deeper irritation, the inexplicable aversion he held for the mystical elements that seemed to entwine Elders Rest and his distrust and dislike of Agnes.

Belladonna slipped silently away; her mission of subtle intervention accomplished. David brushed off the encounter with a dismissive shake. He didn't want Rose to see his reaction to the cat, even though he had been sorely tempted to give it another quick kick. Unbeknownst to him, the enigmatic cat had become an inadvertent player in the unfolding mystery, a guardian of secrets that transcended both time and the petty dislikes of a witchfinder.

***

Jane stood in the shadows, her eyes narrowed as she watched the interaction between Rose and the witchfinder, David, a man she had decided she wanted, given his attraction and power. She couldn't deny the pang of jealousy that gnawed at her heart as she observed the way he looked at the young woman, his eyes alight with a hunger that made her skin crawl. David seemed to be drawn to Rose like a moth to a flame, his attentions bordering on obsession, and Jane couldn't bear to watch when she wanted to become the object of his affection. Clutching her apron tightly in her hands, Jane seethed with resentment as she plotted her revenge. She knew she couldn't compete with Rose's beauty, but she could still make her pay for stealing the attention of the man she desired.

Later that day Jane found David outside the kitchen. She stood before him, her heart pounding with a mixture of anticipation and dread. She had finally worked up the courage to approach him, hoping to win his favour and secure her place by his side. But as she looked into his eyes, she saw only disdain reflected at her.

"I have something to offer you" she began, "something that could be of great use to you and maybe great comfort too." David raised an eyebrow, his expression unreadable. "And what might that be?"

Jane touched his arm and whispered "I could be of great comfort to you during the cold nights, but also, I know things, secrets that could be valuable to someone in your position. I could help you in your endeavors if only you would give me the chance." For a moment, there was silence between them as David regarded her with a cold detachment. Then, without warning, he let out a harsh laugh that sent a shiver down Jane's spine.

"You?" he scoffed; his lip curled in disgust. "And what exactly do you have to offer, with your pockmarked face and your lowly station?"

Jane felt a surge of anger rise within her, but she quickly stifled it, forcing herself to maintain her composure even though his words stung like a slap in the face.

"I may not have the beauty of some" she replied through gritted teeth, but I have loyalty and a willingness to serve you." But David's expression remained unchanged, his gaze cold and indifferent as he regarded her with thinly veiled contempt.

"I do not need someone like you," he said dismissively. "You may go now, and do not bother me with your foolishness again." Jane turned and hurried away, consumed by bitterness and resentment.

Later that day in the dimly lit kitchen, Jane stealthily retrieved a small pouch containing blue cohosh, a potent herb known for its causative properties. She slipped some of this herb into the tea she was making for Lady Harrington. She was consumed with hatred and bitterness and still reeling from the words of the witchfinder and she knew that the effects of this herb could be catastrophic. Satisfied with her treacherous deed Jane hurriedly returned the pouch to its hiding place and resumed her duties in serving the tea, a malicious glint in her eye.

Chapter Thirteen
2023

The following morning, after a somewhat restless sleep, Jess took her coffee into the living room. As she sat on the settee, the old recipe book was on the coffee table in front of her.
Should she attempt to have another look through it for more clues, or should she wait for Edward? He was teaching that day and wouldn't be home until after 4 pm. Restless she got up and decided to call Frank and see if he knew anyone who would come over and look at the fireplace for her, she still hadn't managed to get it working and was thinking about having the wood burner removed and making the hearth into an open fire. She had fond memories of an open fire and loved the warmth and homeliness it would give to the cottage.

She glanced at the bookcase which stood beside the large hearth. That might need removing or moving. It had been there as long as she could remember and maybe longer. Her grandmother was very fond of the bookcase, and it still had some old books there from many years ago, yellowing and musty and probably some would be worth money, but Jess couldn't bear to disturb any of them, and she found them aesthetically pleasing and in keeping with the cottage. She also knew that it was time she decided what to do about the Bistro. In her heart, she knew that she should sell it and maybe with the money she could start something again, here in Harrop Fold or the surrounding area where she now knew that she wanted to stay. She resolved to talk to an Estate Agent that day and get things moving. She thought about Edward then, and she could feel butterflies in her stomach. He was very attractive, and she did feel that they had a connection that she hoped would develop further. Even though after her last relationship she had vowed never to get involved with anyone and just concentrate on her business, she felt that Edward was somehow special. She already felt like she had known him for years, which of course she hadn't but somehow, he just felt right. She smiled to herself and went into the kitchen to do some baking.

She was going to make a Lancashire Parkin (+) and she didn't need the old recipe book, but she had it in the kitchen just in case.

As she embarked on the task of making the cake, the aroma of sweet ingredients filled Elders Rest. The rhythmic blending of flour and eggs became a soothing melody, casting a sense of normality amidst the unfolding mysteries.

With flour-dusted hands and a heart full of curiosity, Jess embraced the therapeutic art of baking. The kitchen became a haven, and the scent of ginger and spices wafted through the air. As the cake batter came together, Jess's mind drifted to Elders Rest's history. Bella suddenly jumped onto the counter, knocking off the old recipe book which opened as it fell to the floor. Jess tutted and picked it up to put it back on the old kitchen table.

In a moment suspended between the mixing bowl and the oven's warmth, Jess found herself standing on a cobbled path that led to Harrington Hall.

She could see David, the witchfinder, a sinister figure with a cloak billowing in the breeze, walking alongside Rose toward the hall. The shadows cast by the towering trees seemed to dance in sync with their footsteps. As Jess observed the witchfinder's face, a chill ran down her spine. His features bore an uncanny resemblance to the clockmaker, Philip. The same piercing gaze and sharp contours seemed to bridge the centuries, creating a disconcerting connection between the two figures. A black cat padded silently beside them, a replica of Bella. The cat's emerald eyes gleamed with an otherworldly knowing, mirroring the timeless quality that transcended the boundaries of time. *They seemed to* be *having a rather intense conversation, but Jess couldn't make out the words and as the vision began to fade, she thought she could see another figure in the background. Suddenly, the vision shifted and she was in the kitchen but not her own. This was a large kitchen with a huge fireplace and pots and pans hanging from the ceiling and a chicken roasting over the fire. She could see a servant girl making tea, but as she looked closer, she could see that this girl was putting something in the tea. It looked like a herb of some kind. The girl turned and looked in Jess's direction. Jess gasped at the pure evil in the eyes that caught hers. She dropped the spoon she was holding and as she bent to retrieve it, the vision faded away.*

Jess stood in her kitchen; the mixing spoon frozen in her hand. The revelation hit her like a wave. The witchfinder and Philip shared not only a physical resemblance but also a connection that echoed through the ages. Elders Rest held secrets that intertwined the destinies of those who walked its cobbled paths, both in the past and the present. In the silence of the kitchen, with the scent of baking enveloping her, Jess grappled with the enigma that Elders Rest presented. An enigma that wove together the threads of history, magic, and an old grandfather clock that ticked not just in seconds but across centuries. Putting the cake to cool, Jess made the sudden decision to go and see the clockmaker, Philip. She knew he had a workshop in Slaidburn, which was a village very near Harrop Fold.

As she ventured into Slaidburn's winding streets, she felt an unshakable pull toward Philip's workshop. The ticking of clocks became a rhythmic guide, leading her to the unassuming house of the clockmaker. Pushing open the door, a small bell chimed softly, announcing Jess's entrance. Philip, hunched over a disassembled antique clock, looked up with a genial smile that belied the darkness lurking beneath.

"Good afternoon, Jess. What brings you back so soon?" he enquired; his eyes gleaming with a subtle intensity. Jess hesitated, glancing around the cluttered shop. The steady tick-tock of various timepieces echoed in the room, creating an eerie backdrop to their conversation. "Philip, we need to talk" she began, her voice steady but determined.

Philip, feigning innocence, responded with practiced ease. "Of course, Jess, is it the clock, has it stopped working again?".

"No, the clock is fine it's about the old recipe book you found when you were mending it," Jess replied.

Philip sighed and Jess could sense that he didn't want to discuss anything with her and she was sure it was because of the book. She pressed on, recounting the visions she had experienced whilst reading the pages of the old recipe book. Philip's eyes flickered with an intensity that betrayed an awareness of more than he let on.

"You mentioned something about the book being a book of shadows? Jess repeated what he had said at the time. Philip stared at her intently with his pale grey eyes and then laughed,

"No, I was just pulling your leg, Jess. I'm sure it's nothing more than an old recipe book and your visions are probably nothing more than dreams. I do believe that there are such things as "A Book of Shadows" or spell books but I am sure that your recipe book is just that and nothing more. I am quite busy Jess, so I will need to get on if that's ok?"

They continued chatting for a few minutes about more mundane subjects, but Jess could sense that Philip was avoiding the subject of the book. The air in the room crackled with an unspoken tension and Jess couldn't shake the feeling that Philip wasn't telling the truth. Unbeknownst to Jess, once she left the shop, a sinister smile played on Philip's lips, revealing his true intentions and a malevolent gleam in his eyes.

***

As the clock struck midnight, Philip sat alone in his dimly lit workshop, surrounded by the comforting tick-tock of the timepieces he tended to. However, tonight there was no solace to be found in the familiar rhythm. His mind was consumed with thoughts of Elders Rest, the old book, and Jess. Ever since he had laid eyes on the book, he had been haunted with an inexplicable compulsion to possess it. At first, he dismissed it as mere curiosity but as the days went by the pull was growing stronger, gnawing at the edges of his sanity.

Tonight, the feeling was overwhelming and as a wave of dizziness washed over him images flashed before his eyes; visions of a shadowy figure cloaked in darkness. It was as if an unseen force held him captive, dragging him deeper into the abyss. He could see the shadowy figure before him and feel its malevolent presence, its tendrils twisting and coiling around his thoughts, threatening to consume him whole.

"Fight it" Philip whispered to himself, his voice barely a breath against the overwhelming darkness. He tried not to think of the book but with each passing moment the lines between reality and delusion blurred. Suddenly a voice pierced through the dark, a voice that was not his own but one that resonated with an ancient power.

"Embrace it", the voice hissed dripping with malice and deceit. "Embrace the darkness within you and you shall wield power beyond imagining. You must take the book back ". Philip's head spun and he didn't know whether he wanted the book out of compulsion or desire. The shadowy figure receded but Philip remained haunted by the vision. Shadows still clouded his mind but he resolved to get the "Book of Shadows" whatever the cost.

Chapter Fourteen
1612
Six Months Later

In the hallowed halls of Harrington Hall, the air was thick with the anticipation of a momentous event. Lady Harrington, her delicate frame ensconced in a canopy bed adorned with rich fabrics, faced the delicate dance between life and death. Agnes stood vigil, her presence both comforting and enigmatic. Rose was helping by bringing towels and water and making sure there was plenty of hot tea. The chamber was steeped in a haunting stillness as Lady Harrington's laboured breaths synchronized with the rhythmic cadence of Agnes' silent vigil. The moon cast an ethereal glow through the ornate curtains, lending an otherworldly quality to the birthing chamber.

Downstairs in the library Lord Harrington was drinking a large glass of wine and pacing the floor, his need for an heir uppermost in his mind.

"Agnes, "Lady Harrington whispered, her voice fraught with a blend of anticipation and fear. "I can feel the presence of my future in this room". Agnes, her eyes carrying the weight of ancient knowledge, nodded solemnly, offering a reassuring touch to Lady Harrington's trembling hand. The other servants moved with practiced grace, the air thick with the scent of herbs and the quietude of centuries-old secrets.

    Lady Harrington lay on her bed, her face pale and drawn with exhaustion. The room was hushed, the only sounds were the soft rustle of fabric as Agnes moved about attending to her. Rose stood in the background her fists clenched with tension as she watched her mother's every move. In the dim light of the chamber, Lady Harrington's features were etched with pain as she struggled through each contraction. Her breath came in ragged gasps, her brow furrowed with the effort of bringing new life into the world.

    Finally, after what felt like an eternity, there was a moment of eerie stillness. Agnes's hands stilled; her gaze fixed on the tiny form cradled in her arms. Rose held her breath, her heart pounding as Lady Harrington looked at Agnes waiting for the sound of her child's first cry. But there was a deathly silence, broken only by the soft murmur of Agnes's voice as she whispered a prayer under her breath.

Lady Harrington's eyes filled with tears as she reached out to touch the tiny bundle in the midwife's arms. Her heart ached with grief too profound for words as she realized that her child, a boy, would never draw breath, never know the warmth of her embrace.

"He was meant to be the heir," Lady Harrington murmured, her voice a delicate thread holding back the torrent of grief threatening to engulf her. Agnes, her wise gaze softened with empathy, responded, "Fate weaves its own design, my lady. Some threads are beyond our control."

"Leave me alone please, everyone please leave" Lady Harrington was distraught taking big breaths as she gulped back the tears that fell relentlessly down her face.
"Just leave me with Margaret my maid and please go, all of you."

Margaret, Lady Harrington's personal lady's maid, had lingered at the periphery, drawn by the gravity of the scene, her eyes fixed on the emotional tableau unfolding before her.

***

Moments later when everyone had gone, Lady Harrington, weakened by grief and desperation, found herself confiding in the unsuspecting maid.

"It's my fault," she said quietly.

"No, my lady, sometimes fate is against us. The poor little mite just wasn't strong enough, you did nothing wrong." Margaret laid a hand on Lady Harrington trying in some way to offer comfort.

"I took a potion" Lady Harrington confessed, her voice barely above a whisper." "Agnes gave it to me. I thought it would ensure a healthy birth, a future for Harrington Hall."

Margaret's eyes widened with a mixture of shock and intrigue. "A potion? You mean…witchcraft?"

Lady Harrington nodded; guilt etched across her features. "Desperation led me to seek remedies beyond our understanding. Now I fear the consequences."

As the news of the stillborn child echoed through the corridors of Harrington Hall and reached the kitchen, Jane's heart pounded erratically within her chest. She stood amongst the bustling chaos of the kitchen, her hands trembling with a mixture of guilt and apprehension. The air felt heavy with tension, each whispered conversation and furtive glance weighing down on her conscience like an anchor. A twisted smile tugged at the corners of Jane's lips as she watched the servants exchange worried glances and murmured hushed prayers for the grieving Lady Harrington. Deep within the recesses of her mind a voice whispered darkly urging her to revel in the chaos she alone had wrought. The realization of her actions sent a shiver down her spine, leaving her cold and hollow inside. However, she realized that no one was aware of the sinister role she had played in the tragedy that had befallen her mistress and she knew that her revenge on Agnes and Rose would be completed sooner than she had anticipated.

***

Downstairs, in the opulent chambers of Lord Harrington, the air hung heavy with the scent of anticipation. The flickering candles cast wavering shadows, adding a surreal quality to the solemn occasion. Winthrop, the butler, bearing news as delicate as glass, approached the formidable figure of Lord Harrington.

"My Lord," he hesitated, sensing the gravity of the words he carried, "I regret to inform you...the child...he did not survive."
Lord Harrington turned from the window, "I have a son?"

Winthrop cleared his throat, "Yes, my Lord but he didn't survive, I am so very sorry".

Time seemed to hang suspended, the words echoing through the chamber like a mournful dirge. Lord Harrington, a stoic figure accustomed to command, felt the foundations of his world crumble beneath the weight of the devastating news. A heavy silence enveloped the room, broken only by the distant howl of the wind outside. Lord Harrington's eyes, once steely and resolute, now betrayed a vulnerability that had long been concealed beneath the façade of authority.

"What do you mean…did not survive?" Lord Harrinton's voice, though measured, carried an undercurrent of disbelief.

Winthrop, for once avoiding direct eye contact, stammered, "I... I'm afraid, my lord, the child was stillborn. Lady Harrington is grieving in her chambers."

The news struck Lord Harrington like a thunderbolt, a visceral pain that transcended the confines of reason. The candlelight flickered as if mirroring the tumult within his soul. The heir, the promise of continuity, the embodiment of generations past and futures unwritten shattered in the cold grip of destiny.

"Leave me" Lord Harrington commanded; his voice strained. The butler withdrew silently, leaving the lord to confront the devastating reality in solitude. Alone in the dimly lit chamber, Lord Harrington allowed the weight of grief to wash over him. The flickering candles cast dancing shadows on the portraits of ancestors lining the walls, each seeming to bear witness to the rupture in the lineage they had forged. A solitary tear traced its path down Lord Harrington's cheek, a testament to the vulnerability beneath the armour of nobility. In that solitary moment, Harrington Hall, once a bastion of certainty, stood on the precipice of uncertainty, its lord grappling with the profound loss that would echo through the annals of his lineage.

Upstairs, Lady Harrington prostate with grief, dismissed Margaret from her chambers, but unbeknownst to her, the words exchanged in that shadowed chamber would cast ripples far beyond the confines of Harrington Hall.

***

In the hours that followed, as whispers of Lady Harrington's stillborn child spread through the servant corridors, the information reached the ears of the Witchfinder-David Walker, a sinister figure whose presence loomed over the valley like a harbinger of malevolence. The moon, indifferent to human drama, bore silent witness to the unraveling tapestry of secrets and sorrows, leaving Harrington Hall forever marked by the echoes of grief and the ominous designs of those who sought to exploit its vulnerabilities.

Chapter Fifteen
2023

The aroma of steak and onions slowly cooking wafted through the air of Jess's cozy kitchen, a haven where the flavours unfolded beneath the steady hands of a culinary artist. Jess, apron-clad and fully immersed in her cooking had decided to treat herself and Edward to a Steak and Stilton Pie (+). She didn't need a recipe for this as she had made it many times and consequently had decided not to give in to the temptation of looking through the old recipe book. As the Aga emanated warmth, Jess's hands moved with practiced grace. The sizzle of garlic and herbs and the rhythmic chopping of vegetables became a culinary symphony, a therapeutic diversion from the mysteries and burdens that haunted her thoughts. She had put the bistro on the market that morning and had felt much lighter in her mind now that she had made the decision. She was going to look for new premises in Clitheroe or maybe one of the surrounding villages and open a bistro/café once again. She had talked this over with Edward and they were going to look together at the weekend. She smiled when she thought of Edward. They had kissed last night and although they were both taking things very slowly, she had a good feeling and felt almost as if she had known him all her life. She was very comfortable with him, and they shared the same interests, and these visions of Agnes and Rose had brought them closer.

Once the pie was crafted to perfection, Jess carefully placed it in the oven, allowing the savoury masterpiece to undergo its transformative journey into a golden-brown revelation. The tantalizing scents filled the kitchen, wrapping Jess in a cocoon of culinary contentment. With the pie in the oven Jess turned her attention once again to the old recipe book. She gently caressed its worn cover, a silent acknowledgment of the timeless secrets it held. As she closed the book, an inexplicable compulsion guided her to the bookcase. The book found its resting place, nestled among its literary companions. Yet, as Jess stood before the bookcase, there was a sudden shift in the air, and through a veil of mist she could see the ethereal figure of a servant from Harrington Hall approaching the cottage. As she watched, she was there beside Agnes as the servant opened the door.

Margaret's eyes mirrored the anxiety that gripped her heart. Her face etched with fear and determination as she approached Elder's Rest where she knew Agnes resided. The weight of unspoken words hung heavy in the air, as if the very walls of Elder's Rest were privy to the tidings of doom that Margaret bore. Margaret pushed open the door of the cottage which was slightly ajar. She could see Agnes by the fireplace. "Agnes," she whispered, "Agnes, they're coming for you?"

Agnes turned around, her green eyes luminous in the shadows of the cottage.

"Who is, Margaret?" she said with a lot more confidence than she felt.

"They know about the potion Agnes" Margaret's voice trembled. "I'm sorry but up at the Hall they know, and Lord Harrington is calling you a witch. I think the witchfinder is on his way here. I had to warn you".

Agnes felt her heart race and she found she was trembling slightly. "I've done nothing wrong Margaret, let them come. I am a healer, not a witch and my potion had nothing to do with that poor little soul not making it into this world."

Margaret looked at Agnes with sorrow and fear. "Lord Harrington is in an awful rage; I fear for you".

"Thank you for coming Margaret but you may leave, please. I am not afraid of Lord Harrington or that weasel of a witchfinder, I believe in my healing abilities, and I have never done anyone any harm. Go now, before they arrive." Agnes said bravely.

As she left Agnes closed the door to the cottage. Elders Rest was once a haven but would soon be besieged by the relentless forces of accusation. As she went about her business, she had no idea of the horrors that were to follow.

As the vision dissipated, leaving Jess rooted in the present, the scent of the Steak and Stilton Pie filled the kitchen. However, the culinary respite stood juxtaposed against the foreboding echoes of Margaret's footsteps and the spectral revelation that foretold of imminent storms gathering over Elder's Rest. So, the baby did not survive, and Agnes was going to be blamed because of the potion. Was this why Agnes disappeared and then Rose was accused of witchcraft? She sat quietly for a minute, always slightly dizzy and confused as these visions came and then just as quickly vanished.

Jess resolved to talk to Edward later that day about her vision but in the meantime, she had a builder coming over to look at the fireplace and discuss her options about opening it up into a working fireplace to replace the wood burner. She glanced over at the bookcase to the old recipe book which was nestled amongst the old books and noticed that Bella was sleeping on top of one of the upper shelves. She smiled at the old cat and giving her a quick stroke, she went to get changed before the arrival of the builder.

***

As Jess stood by the kitchen window, gazing out at the tranquil countryside bathed in sunshine, she couldn't shake the feeling of restlessness gnawing at her soul. The familiar sights and sounds of Harrop Fold offered little solace as her mind wandered back to memories she had long tried to bury. Leaning against the cool stone wall, Jess closed her eyes, letting the memories flood her mind like a tidal wave crashing against the shore. She could still feel the warmth of his touch, hear the echoes of his laughter, and see the intensity of his eyes as they locked gazes. But along with the bittersweet reminiscence came the sting of regret, the ache of heartbreak, and the weight of unanswered questions that lingered like shadows in the recesses of her mind. The breakup with Greg had affected her deeply. She had thought she had moved on, built walls around her heart to shield herself from the pain of the past, but today those walls felt fragile, crumbling under the weight of unresolved emotions.

A soft sigh escaped her lips as she wrestled with the conflicting emotions swirling within her. On the one hand, there was the pull of nostalgia, the longing for the familiarity and comfort of what once was. On the other hand, there was the stark reality of the present, the uncertainty of the future, and the fear of opening old wounds that had never fully healed.

Lost in her thoughts, Jess didn't hear the soft footsteps approaching from behind until a gentle hand came to rest on her shoulder, pulling her back to the present. She turned to see Edward standing there, his eyes filled with concern and understanding.

"Are you alright Jess?" he asked, his voice soft and reassuring.

Jess hesitated for a moment, grappling with the urge to confide in him, to bare her soul and share the burden weighing heavily on her heart. But the words caught in her throat, and instead, she offered him a faint smile, masking the turmoil raging within.

"I'm fine, Edward" she replied, her voice barely above a whisper. "Just lost in thought, I suppose."

Edward studied her for a moment, his gaze searching hers as if trying to unravel the mysteries hidden behind her eyes. And although Jess longed to let him in, to allow herself to be vulnerable in his presence, she couldn't shake the fear of what lay dormant below the surface.

With a gentle squeeze of her hand, Edward nodded, his silent support a beacon of light in the darkness that threatened to consume her. As they stood together, bathed in the soft glow of the afternoon sun, Jess couldn't help but wonder if someday she would find the courage to confront the ghosts of her past and finally lay them to rest.

Chapter Sixteen
1612

In the dimly lit library of Harrington Hall, Lord Harrington sat in contemplative solitude. The grandeur of his ancestral home provided little solace as the echoes of unsettling revelations reverberated within. David Walker, the Witchfinder, stood before him, a bearer of truths that would shatter the veneer of domestic tranquility.

"Lord Harrington," Walker's voice, a harbinger of disquiet, sliced through the silence", there are veils of deceit that cloak the heart of your household".

The Lord's gaze, once steadfast, now flickered with uncertainty. "Speak plainly, Walker. I will not tolerate riddles in my own home."

David looked at him, his pale grey eyes shining with malevolence. "Your lady, Lady Harrington, sought the aid of Agnes of Elder's Rest. A potion, brewed with the promise of life, was consumed to quicken her womb." Lord Harrington's stern countenance hardened as he stared at the Witchfinder.

"The potion, however, then yielded a somber harvest," Walker continued, his words laden with an unspeakable weight. "The child did not draw breath. As you are aware, Lady Harrington's womb cradled a stillborn son."

As the truth hung in the air, a storm brewed within Lord Harrington, an amalgamation of grief, betrayal, and a sense of marital trust fractured beyond repair. The Lord's eyes, once a reflection of paternal pride, now brimmed with a mixture of sorrow and ire. "My wife," he uttered with a tremor, "she sought this potion without my knowledge?"

The Witchfinder nodded solemnly. "The roots of Elders Rest and Agnes intertwine with mysteries that may defy mortal comprehension. The very essence of its offerings is entwined with forces beyond the knowledge of man. I very much fear that we are looking at witchcraft, here at Harrington Hall and within these villages."

Lord Harrington stood up, his anger palpable in his stance. "What folly is this, Walker? you are talking in riddles again. Agnes is a mere healer, a guardian of herbal remedies. Lady Harrington would not involve herself in such superstitious practices." His voice was laced with a defensive edge.

"Her maid, Margaret has told that Lady Harrington confessed this to her" David unyielding in his conviction, then produced an empty vial. "This was found by the maid in her Ladyships chambers. This is the evidence of her transgressions. The potion that binds her fate with the alleged witchcraft of Elders Rest.".

As Lord Harrington stared at the vial, a tempest of conflicting emotions churned within him.

"What would you have me do?" Lord Harrington's voice, a mixture of frustration and uncertainty, betrayed the cracks in his authoritative façade.

"We must confront the source of this malevolence," the Witchfinder declared, his eyes fixed on Lord Harrington. "Elders Rest and the witch Agnes harbour secrets that threaten the very fabric of your lineage. The witchcraft that festers within its walls must be expunged for the preservation of your family's honour."

Lord Harrington banged loudly on the table with both fists.

"Go, go and get this wretched woman and bring her to me, I need to speak to my wife. Don't come back without her. "Lord Harrington dismissed the witchfinder and walked purposely up to his wife's bed-chamber, anger simmering below the surface.

As the Witchfinder left the Hall, a storm began to rage both outside and within.
***

Lord Harrington, his countenance etched with a mixture of anguish and stern resolve, approached Lady Harrington. The flickering candlelight cast dancing shadows on the walls, mirroring the tumultuous emotions that swirled within.

"Evelyn," Lord Harrington's voice, usually a pillar of authority, now quivered with the anguish of a betrayed heart. "What treachery is this? Evelyn, did you seek a potion from Agnes of Elders Rest. The midwife that attended you?" his question hung in the air, a thread that threatened to unravel the carefully woven tapestry of marital trust.

Lady Harrington, her eyes reflecting a mix of guilt and vulnerability, met his gaze with a heavy heart. Her gaze faltered, and after a moment of silence that felt like an eternity, she nodded, a silent admission that reverberated in the dimness of the chamber. Lord Harrington unmoved by her tears continued

"The witchfinder spoke of a potion, a concoction that promised life. But the child, our child Evelyn, did not draw one breath. Is this your doing?" spittle was forming at the sides of his mouth. Evelyn had never seen him so angry.

With tears streaming down her face, Evelyn nodded once again. "I am sorry my Lord, I thought it would help, but I have let you down."

Lord Harrington swung round to face his wife.

"I have sent for the witch Agnes to see what she has to say and will deal with her accordingly. As for you, you are to go to my sisters in Skipton and remain there until I have purged this village of sorcery. I can't bear to look at you right now. I know you are grieving, as am I, but until this matter is sorted with Agnes and this potion I would rather that you weren't here"

Lord Harrington stormed out slamming the door. Evelyn rested her head on her arms and wept. Never had she felt so wretched. She had lost her child, now she was losing her husband. She should never have taken that potion. She may have to go to Skipton, but she too would make sure that Agnes paid for what she had done.

Chapter Seventeen
2023

The morning sun cast a warm glow over Elders Rest, as Jess welcomed the local builder, a seasoned craftsman known for his expertise in restoring historic structures, in particular fireplaces and their surrounds. As the builder, a man named Thomas examined the hearth, his weathered hands traced the contours of the ancient stones. His brow furrowed in concentration, a silent conversation between craftsman and artifact.

"Well," he said to Jess, there's no problem taking the wood burner out, but to make this a proper working fireplace we will have to expand it and clean the chimney. However, your main problem is the bookcase."

"Oh no, why" Jess was beginning to look worried; she didn't want to move or disturb the bookcase that had been a feature for so long.

Thomas looked at her sympathetically.

"I know I'm sorry, but it is built into the very structure of the hearth. I can't even start to take the wood burner out without removing the bookcase."

Jess felt a shiver as if someone had walked over her grave, even making her turn round, but there was nothing there, only Bella on the chair in the corner, her emerald eyes fixed with a glare at Thomas, the builder. Jess hesitated for a moment, her eyes scanning the collection of books and trinkets that adorned the shelves. Each item told a story, and the prospect of disrupting this arrangement felt like disturbing the dormant echoes of time.

"Can it be done without damaging anything?" Jess asked.

Thomas nodded reassuringly. "Oh absolutely. We'll handle it with care. Once we've sorted out the hearth, we can find a new place for this beauty, it might even enhance its charm in a different corner of your cottage."

Jess thought about it for a second. "Okay, let's do it, when do you think you can start?"

Thomas consulted a small diary he had. In the next day or two, but it's going to be a bit of a mess, have you anywhere you can stay "?

"Yes, she can stay with me," said a deep voice from the doorway, as Edward walked in.

Jess turned and smiled, her heart missing a beat at the sight of his lovely face. Just as she was about to reply, Frank walked through the door too.

"Well, it's all go here today," he remarked. "Jess, I have something to discuss with you, and maybe Edward too, if you have five minutes?"

Thomas gathered his things and left the cottage, promising Jess, he would telephone her later that day with a definite date.

Jess went to make coffee and the three of them sat around the old kitchen table.

"I've made a decision" Frank began. "I've decided I'm going to sell the old barn at the top of the lane. It's been fully re-roofed and the walls are sound. I don't use it and I wondered if maybe you would like first refusal? Maybe for a café or something…" he grinned.

Jess and Edward looked at each other. "Wow" Jess exclaimed, can we come over now and look." "Of course, my dears, let's go now and then I'll come back and have some of that delicious-smelling coffee." Frank got up and went to the door. He turned and laughed as Bella leapt of the chair and followed. "Looks like Bella is coming too, that must be a good sign."

As the three of them walked over to the barn, Jess gazed around her. The area was stunning. Miles and miles of green fields and the fells in the distance with their tall pine trees and undulating hills. She noticed a herd of deer on one of the top fields and smiled to herself. She loved it here and if she could start a business too, what could be better?

The outside of the barn was in perfect condition. As Frank had said it had been completely re-roofed with original grey slates and the stonework was immaculate whilst still in keeping with the age. There was a large barn door at the entrance which looked out onto the countryside with panoramic views all around. The inside was still as it would have been with the individual stalls and even some of the brasses and ties that would have been used for animals. The floor was stone and had the original grooves to get rid of waste and the upper level which would have been a hay loft was all timbered and would make an amazing mezzanine floor. Suddenly Jess could see a café or bistro, with a separate bakery, it was certainly large enough. It was also in an ideal spot, being right in the middle of several local footpaths, and would be a haven for walkers.

Having looked all around, Jess turned to Edward and Frank.

"Would you mind if I just had five minutes on my own here".

"Not at all" Frank looked at Edward. "Come on lad let's get that coffee".

They looked at Bella who had sat beside Jess and had decided to stay too.

As they left Jess gazed around her. It was perfect. She stooped down and stroked Bella's head. As she looked up, out of the barn door, and over to the fell, she could have sworn she saw the solitary figure of the young girl with long red hair staring at the barn. When she looked again, she was gone. Jess and Bella walked slowly back to Elders Rest, Jess deep in thought. Suddenly, the wind seemed to pick up and it started to rain. As Jess hurried to the door, her vision blurred.

The lane that was concrete was now cobbled and there were no streetlights. There was thunder and a flash of lightning and she could see a man all dressed in black with a billowing cloak, carrying some sort of tall stick moving silently and malevolently towards the cottage door.

Jess gasped and cried out, and Bella hissed and arched her back.

For a second it seemed that the man turned and stared straight at Jess with piercing soulless pale grey eyes before he turned, intent on his purpose.

"Jess, are you ok, are you coming in" Edward called from the doorway. Jess looked around, the cobbles had gone, and the sun was shining once again. Jess walked forward but she had an ominous feeling that something was wrong, and she resolved to get the recipe book back out and see if she could find out more.

Jess's hands sifted through the shelves in the cozy living room of Elders Rest, panic clawing at her as the realization set in. The old recipe book was nowhere to be found. Her heart raced, and a cold sweat broke out on her forehead. The book, the key to unlocking the mysteries of the past, had vanished without a trace.

Frustration and desperation etched on her face as she rushed into the kitchen of Higher Harrop Fold Farm where Frank had returned after having his coffee with Edward.

"Frank, have you seen the old recipe book? I can't find it anywhere," she blurted out, her voice tinged with anxiety.

Frank, a reassuring presence with his weathered face and kind eyes, furrowed his brow. "No, lass, I haven't touched it. Why don't you ask Philip? He was here earlier to check on the clock like you asked him to."

Jess's eyes widened at the mention of the clockmaker. "I didn't ask him to check on the clock" "she screamed in frustration. "Get Edward quickly we're going to see Philip now."

***

Upon arriving, the shop door swung open with a gentle jingle, but there was no sign of Philip.

They all shouted for him and heard a weak voice coming from the back room. On finding him Jess immediately confronted him about the missing book, her voice tinged with accusation.

"Philip, where is the old recipe book? Frank said you came to the cottage" she demanded.

Philip, looking pale and visibly shaken, stammered out an explanation.

"It's over there on the table. I'm sorry I took it. I don't know... it was as if something or someone was making me take it. As I reached out for it Bella your cat scratched me and I've started feeling strange ever since, I'm so sorry." Jess rushed over to the table to retrieve the book, still angry with Philip for taking it.

Edward's eyes narrowed as he observed the clockmaker's uneasy demeanor.

"Jess look at his face. That's not just a scratch. He's reacting." The realization hit Jess like a wave. Philip must have been allergic to cats and had fallen victim to Bella's claws. Anaphylactic shock gripped him, evident in his swollen face and laboured breathing.

Panicking, Jess dialed for emergency assistance, while Frank rushed to get an EpiPen from the nearby pharmacy. As the ambulance raced towards Slaidburn, Philip's face grew more distorted, and the urgency of the situation hung heavy in the air.

Chapter Eighteen
1612

The hamlet of Harrop Fold lay quiet under the dappled moonlight although a storm was brewing, and the wind had begun to howl. David Walker strode purposefully toward Elders Rest Cottage. As he approached the ancient cottage, his keen senses detected the presence of another. Through the ethereal glow of the night and the rain which had started to fall, he discerned the silhouette of a young woman, a figure he recognized as Rose, on her way to Elders Rest.

"Rose," he called out, his voice cutting through the stillness like a blade. "What brings you to this place at such an hour?" Rose turned to face him, her eyes reflecting a mixture of defiance and trepidation. "I have matters to discuss with my mother, matters that do not concern you, Witchfinder." David's sinister grin widened, fueled by the arrogance of his assumed authority. "Matters that may become easier if you choose to cooperate, my dear. The path you tread will lead to accusations and trials. However, I can make it all disappear, if you allow me to. We never did finish our earlier discussion, did we?"

He advanced, a predator closing in on its prey, and reached out to touch Rose's cheek. However, she stepped back, her resolve unbroken.

"Your promises carry no weight here. Leave me be, I have already told you I am courting and I have no interest in you. Undeterred, David persisted. He moved even closer, attempting to force a kiss upon her, but Rose, fueled by a strength born of defiance and revulsion, resisted. Unbeknownst to either of them, Bella materialized from the shadows.

The air crackled with tension as Rose, her eyes aflame with determination, spoke.

"I will not succumb to your darkness Witchfinder. I will not bow to your tyranny or succumb to your evil thoughts". Rose struck him hard across the face with all her strength. As David, stung by rejection and reeling slightly from the blow, recoiled, Bella leaped into action. With feline grace, the black cat launched itself at the Witchfinder, claws unsheathed. Amongst the hisses and yowls that pierced the night, Bella scratched the Witchfinder's face, drawing blood. Rose took the opportunity to run, but instead of going to the cottage she fled back to the hall where she thought she would be safer, resolving to see her mother first thing in the morning. She didn't think the witchfinder in the storm and with the bad cut on his face would continue his vengeful path to the cottage.

***

The storm, a tempest of both nature and fate, raged on as David Walker pressed forward toward Elders Rest Cottage. The wind howled through the twisted branches of ancient trees, and rain lashed against the roofs of centuries-old dwellings. But David's fury stoked by rejection and the pain of Bella's attack, burned brighter than the lightning streaking across the darkened sky. His face, marked by the deep cut from Bella's strike, throbbed with pain and indignation and had begun to swell as the feline poison that David was allergic to seeped into his bloodstream. The rain, mingling with his blood, traced crimson rivulets down his swollen cheek. Yet, fueled by a malevolent determination, he brushed aside the discomfort and continued his relentless march.

Bella trailed him from a safe distance, her eyes gleaming like orbs of emerald fire, as Elders Rest loomed ahead, its silhouette barely visible through the veil of thunderous rain and shadows. As David approached, his hands clenched into fists, the storm mirrored the tempest within him. Thunder boomed in harmony with his wrath, and lightning illuminating the path. Upon reaching the threshold, David, cloaked in the storm's fury, raised his hand to knock. The rain, a relentless drumbeat against the door seemed to echo the foreboding rhythm of impending reckoning. As the Witchfinder's hand met the door, the atmosphere tensed, and Elders Rest held its breath, poised at the precipice of a confrontation that would resonate through time.

Chapter Nineteen
2023

Later that evening, when everyone had left, Jess was alone in the cottage. She thought of her vision of the man coming to the door, the same man from earlier visions who was coming for Agnes because of the potion she made. She also thought of her sightings of Rose the girl with the red hair. She had heard that Philip was in hospital and recovering and she resolved to go and see him in a day or two to have a chat about what had happened. Even though she had promised Edward that she wouldn't look at the old recipe book she knew she wouldn't be able to resist. She had also decided that she would finally attempt to make the recipe for Malkin Pie (+).

When Philip had mentioned that the recipe book was a "Book of Shadows" Jess had investigated and discovered that this was a collection of instructions and texts for spells and other practices often associated with witchcraft. This old book was Agnes's personalized journal where she had kept all her knowledge, and it was a compilation of spells, rituals and recipes. She was now convinced that the recipes held the keys to her visions. Jess and Edward had both concluded that the recipe for Malkin Pie could well be the strongest link and although Jess knew it might be unwise to start this on her own, she felt a strong connection to Agnes and Rose and indeed her lovely cottage Elders Rest, so she was determined to find out the truth for herself. She moved into the kitchen and gathered all her ingredients. Bella had positioned herself on top of the fridge and was watching proceedings with her knowing emerald gaze.

It was quite a complicated recipe and she had to compromise on some ingredients and give her interpretation of the actual method of making it but she was excited about the result and soon immersed herself in the joy of creating a delicious savoury pie. As the aromas filled the kitchen and Jess hummed along to the radio, she heard a loud crash from the living room. Bella leapt off the fridge and Jess ran into the next room. As soon as she entered the living room, her vision became hazy and figures seemed to swirl before her very eyes. She could hear the storm and feel the fear and she realized that her living room had transformed and she was back with Agnes.

The witchfinder moved forward. "By the authority vested in me, you are accused of witchcraft and consorting with the devil." He declared, as he stepped in through the door of Elders Rest to confront Agnes as she stood by the fireplace. She turned around, her eyes blazing along with the storm that raged outside. "Get out of my house, you baneful man. I have done nothing wrong, and I am not leaving this cottage, certainly not with you." She took a step back as the witchfinder began to walk towards her. "You have made a pact with the devil and put a curse on Lady Harrington's stillborn child with your evil potions. You will come back to the Hall and face justice" he raged.

Agnes laughed at him and began to turn away. Consumed by righteous fury and fueled by a twisted sense of justice, he lunged at Agnes with an accusatory zeal. The room became a battleground, shadows moving with the frenzied dance of two opposing wills. A resounding slap cut through the air, the echo of betrayal reverberating in the aftermath. Agnes, stunned by the force of the blow, stumbled backward, her hand pressed against her cheek. At that moment, a sinister satisfaction gleamed in David Walker's eyes, a satisfaction that heralded the irreversible descent into malevolence.

As Agnes teetered on the precipice of pain and defiance, a desperate survival instinct ignited within her. In the tumult of the struggle, she reached out for her old recipe book, which was balanced on the bookshelf, and hurled it at the Witchfinder. The storm outside raged in symphony with the chaos within.

In a blind surge of panic and malice, David struck Agnes once more. The force of the blow sent her crashing against the fireplace and her head struck the hearthstone with an ominous thud. As Agnes began to lose consciousness and the blood spilled all around her, she caught sight of Bella in the corner of the room, her green all-knowing eyes bright, her back arched as she watched the horror unfold.

In that moment, David Walker, convinced he had silenced the source of perceived malevolence and the work of the devil then stood frozen in the aftermath of his actions. He had rid the world of one more witch, but what would Lord Harrington say? He had insisted that David return to the Hall with Agnes. How was he going to explain that he had killed her?

David stood over the fallen form of Agnes. Rain soaked, and fevered, he cast a glance around the room until his eyes rested on the bookcase, an unwitting accomplice in the secrets that unfolded within the cottage's ancient walls. Agnes remained still, a silent witness to the storm raging outside and the tempest of human cruelty that had befallen her. As David's ragged breaths filled the room, a sinister realization dawned upon him. The bookcase beckoned with the promise of secrecy. With a determined glint in his eyes, he strode toward the aged wooden structure. He remembered the mechanism, a key to lock away the truth he sought to bury alongside the woman he had felled.

He found the book Precatio Omnium Herbarum and as he pressed on the cover the bookcase swung open revealing the concealed space within it. The flickering light of a lone candle illuminated the cavity, casting eerie shadows that danced upon the ancient stones.

The storm outside continued to rage, as David his features still contorted not only with his efforts but with the cut on his face which was beginning to throb.

He unceremoniously placed the corpse of Agnes in the hidden chamber. As he stood before the hidden compartment within the bookcase, his need for secrecy compelled him to seal the bookcase with a binding force, for even though it could be opened from the outside by pressing on the one book that would open it, he couldn't take that risk.

In the dim light of Elders Rest, he surveyed the room, searching for a means to ensure the secrets he buried remained untouched. His eyes fell upon a small iron box that lay near the fireplace. David opened it and inside nestled amidst moth eaten parchment and worn trinkets, he found a vial of sealing wax. The wax, a dark crimson in the flickering candlelight, promised an unyielding bond. David, driven by the urgency of his actions, melted the wax along the seam of the bookcase and the fireplace. With each twist and stroke, the sealing wax became a sentinel, warding off prying eyes and inquisitive minds and the fate of poor Agnes Thornton who lay entombed.

He replaced all the books, in his haste, ripping a piece of the old book that Agnes had thrown at him. Quickly cleaning up the blood that was congealing on the fireplace he took a final look around the room and at the now sealed bookcase and he hastily made his retreat.

The storm outside raged on as the Witchfinder left to return to the hall, unaware of the torment within the walls of Elders Rest, as Agnes's eyes slowly opened.

***

As the vision gradually cleared, Jess, horrified by what she had seen, stumbled out of Elders Rest, her eyes haunted by the harrowing vision of Agnes's demise. Breathless and disorientated, she clutched the edges of the cottage doorway for support. As she started to cry and scream for Edward, he came running out of the door of Manor House having heard her calls at the same time as Bella flew past him with her tail fluffed out.

"What happened Jess, are you all right?" Edward ran towards her looking worried.

"I…I saw Agnes", Jess stammered, her voice barely audible. "I saw her…her end." Jess was distraught and shaking with tears streaming down her face ". "He killed her" she managed to whisper through her tears.

"Who did?" Edward was trying to make sense of what Jess was saying.

"The Witchfinder. She's behind the bookcase, where he put her and then sealed it shut." Jess was still reeling from her latest vision.

They talked late into the night and gradually even though she was still visibly shaken by what she had seen, Jess calmed down and they began to discuss her plans for the new café, Jess needed to forget about the vision for a while. The barn once converted would make the ideal setting and Jess was very excited about the future. Edward stayed that night and Jess felt a real sense of home and peace and was looking forward to the coming months, although she was now dreading what they might find when the builder dismantled the bookcase.

She was making coffee the following morning and thumbing through the old recipe book. Suddenly as she looked up her vision blurred slightly, and the kitchen faded.

She could see Rose rushing through the cottage, a sense of urgency in her ethereal movements. Rose seemed to be searching for something, her transparent figure disappearing into the darkness before Jess could understand the purpose of her quest, although she now knew that it had something to do with Agnes and she wished with all her heart that she could help.

A few days later, still recovering, Philip reluctantly agreed to meet Jess and Edward in a local village café, "The Old Vicarage" in Tosside. Jess loved this quirky café. It was built within the old vicarage and the dining rooms inside were full of old grandfather clocks and cosy furniture. It served traditional home cooking and had an extensive garden seating area with views over the valley. Jess, armed with a steaming cup of tea, confronted him about the strange events surrounding the disappearance of the old recipe book.

"Philip, we need to understand what happened. Why did you take the book? And why did you seem so angry. It almost as if someone else was guiding you?" Jess enquired, her eyes probing for answers.

Philip hesitated; his gaze fixed on the swirling steam rising from his tea. "Honestly, I don't know. As soon as I entered the cottage it was as if I had been there before and when I found the book, the urge to possess it was so strong. I have no recollection of coming back and taking the book, apart from getting the scratch, I'm so sorry. All I remember is a voice, telling me to get the book."

Edward, ever the pragmatic observer, interjected. "So, you are saying you felt somehow possessed with this obsession to get the book?" Philip nodded, his face haunted with misery.,

"Did you have any idea of the significance of the book Philip", Jess enquired. Philip shook his head. "I've never really believed in anything like that but there is something evil about the book I feel."

Jess and Edward explained to Philip about the old recipe book, Jess's visions, and the terrible end of Anges's life at the hands of David Walker. Philip was understandably distressed but also relieved that although he had played a terrible part in the story, between them all they had at least managed to discover what had happened and the awful act of violence that had occurred in Elders Rest.

Chapter Twenty
1612

As the sealing wax solidified around the door of the hidden compartment, Agnes's world plunged into an inky abyss. The air, now a suffocating embrace, stole her breath, and the crushing darkness pressed against her like an unseen adversary. A primal scream clawed its way up Agnes's throat, a desperate plea for release that reverberated within the sealed chamber. She hammered her fists against the wooden confines, her anguish echoing through the hollowed walls. Yet, the sound morphed into a silent symphony, unheard by the outside world.

Agnes's fingers became desperate claws. Her nails splintered and bloodied as she scraped against the surface, leaving behind marks that mirrored the depths of her torment. In the impenetrable darkness, Agnes's senses heightened. She could feel the vibration of her silent screams, the resonance of her pain echoing through the chamber. Amidst her futile struggle, Agnes's questing hands brushed against an unexpected object. A familiar shape of an old glass bottle that was just within her grasp. Agnes clutched it fervently, the etchings on its surface now a tactile guide in the pitch darkness. The contents within, a potent mixture of needles, pins, rosemary and red wine hummed an ancient magic that seemed to pulse in tandem with Agnes's heartbeat. With the witch's bottle cradled in her hands, Agnes's screams evolved into a muted resilience and her breathing became shallower. A searing pain, not just from the blows she had received but a deeper more profound ache, settled into Agnes's bones.

The bottle was both haunting and comforting. Agnes, while accepting the cruel reality of her entombment, found some solace in the knowledge that she wouldn't be the only one to die that night and that the echoes of these events would reverberate around the villages for a long time to come.

As she desperately tried to open the compartment, she realized that the witchfinder must have sealed the door. Her breathing became shallow, and she kept falling in and out of consciousness. Every time she awoke, she tried again to scream, to scratch at the door but to no avail. Finally, she slept again, only this time she thought she could feel Bella. She could sense her warm presence and eventually after many hours, she silently slipped away with her faithful companion watching over her.

***

As the storm outside Elders Rest howled its lament, the Witchfinder, David emerged from the cottage, his face a twisted mask of pain and frustration. Returning to Harrington Hall, silently followed by a black cat who kept to the shadows, he was summoned to the library, and he found himself under the scrutinizing gaze of Lord Harrington. His patience already worn thin; he confronted David about Agnes's absence. The Witchfinder, feigning ignorance, wove a tale of Agnes's mysterious disappearance, laying the blame on the elusive nature of those accused of witchcraft. Lord Harrington, known for his keen observation, noticed the uncharacteristic pallor that clung to the witchfinders face and the swelling and scratch marks of his confrontation with Bella.

A flicker of suspicion crossed Lord Harrington's eyes.

"So, you couldn't find Agnes. You assume she has disappeared?" "Is Rose her daughter? I believe she is a maid here within the Hall.

"She is my Lord. Her mother has vanished but as kin she should be held accountable", David was beginning to feel very ill and was sweating profusely. Lord Harrington summoned the butler Winthrop.

"Take this man to one of the bedrooms and have someone attend to him, he is clearly unwell" he demanded. "Also summon the household to the library and bring the maid Rose" he demanded. Winthrop scuttled off to do his bidding and David was taken to a bedchamber.

The servants scurried to fulfill the command, but Rose was nowhere to be found within the opulent corridors of the hall. Unbeknownst to Lord Harrington, Rose, driven by an urgency to seek out her mother, had retraced her steps back to the cottage of Elders Rest.

David Walker, the witchfinder, lay in his bed, a grotesque tableau of suffering. The once swollen face now distorted further into a grotesque mask etched with agony. The scratches inflicted by Bella had become festering wounds pulsating with a venom that transcended the mundane. As David gasped for air, the room itself seemed to recoil from the suffocating aura of evil.

Lord Harrington stood by the bedside, his countenance a mixture of fury and fear. The servants were gathered in hushed clusters and exchanged wary glances. Agnes's disappearance and the witchfinders' demise fueled the already rampant whispers of witchcraft that clung to Harrington Hall like a sinister shadow.

David convulsed, the spasms of agony contorting his once robust frame, whilst Bella watched silently from the shadows outside the bedroom window. As David's breaths grew shallow, his eyes, once ablaze with the fervour of persecution, dulled into lifeless orbs. The final gasp escaped his lips, naming Agnes and Rose as witches and carrying with it the echoes of a man consumed by the consequences of his own malevolence. Bella disappeared into the darkness making her way stealthily back across the fells.

In the wake of his demise, a palpable silence descended upon the room. Lord

Harrington, grappling with the inexplicable, cast a suspicious gaze around the chamber.

***

Later Lord Harrington gathered the servants in the grand hall of Harrington Hall. The air was thick with tension, and whispers of witchcraft lingered in the air. As the servants assembled, their expressions ranged from curiosity to trepidation, each bracing for the pronouncements that would resonate through the cavernous halls. Lord Harrington, his countenance etched with a mix of gravity and suspicion, addressed the gathered assembly. His voice, a commanding presence that brooked no dissent, echoed through the hall, cutting through the palpable silence.

"Good servants of Harrington Hall," he began, his words measured and deliberate, "we find ourselves entangled in a web of deceit, where whispers of witchcraft and dark deeds permeate our very walls." A murmur rippled through the assembly. The servants exchanged uneasy glances, acutely aware of the weight that Lord Harrington's words carried.

"I demand your loyalty and cooperation in unraveling the truth" Lord Harrington continued, his eyes scanning the faces before him. "The Witchfinder, in his final moments, accused Agnes and her daughter Rose, of foul sorcery. I seek the truth and I will not tolerate deceit or collusion." "Agnes seems to have disappeared and as for Rose, Lord Harrington's gaze narrowed, "her actions, her loyalties will be scrutinized, and she will be brought before me today."

As Lord Harrington's stern words echoed through the grand hall, a disquieting murmur surged through the servants assembled there. A voice, hesitant at first emerged from the gathered servants. It was Jane, her face twisted with malice.

"Agnes and Rose are witches in our midst. Agnes put a curse on your unborn child and on the witchfinder, both are dead. I say banish the darkness and let justice prevail. If Agnes cannot be found, then Rose must be brought to trial and judgment." she shouted, spittle collecting at the corners of her mouth.

Another voice joined in, "Aye, Rose the daughter is tainted by kin. She should be brought to trial this very day."

Gradually all the servants gathered began to chant the same sentences as fear and suspicion echoed through the grand hall, carrying with it the weight of impending judgement.

Lord Harrington, his stoic façade betraying no emotion, surveyed the chanting servants.

"Go, "he shouted …" Go and bring Rose to me immediately.

Chapter Twenty One
2023

The atmosphere inside Elders Rest was charged with a palpable sense of anticipation as the builder Thomas approached the ancient bookcase. Jess had called him that morning and explained the urgency and had tried to explain what had happened, but she was sure the builder must think she had lost her mind. However, he had agreed to come and dismantle the bookcase that day and to have a look at the barn and give her a quote for the building work that would be necessary to convert it into a café.

Edward, Jess, and Frank watched in silent contemplation; their eyes fixed on the builder's skilled hands as he delicately began the process of dismantling the bookcase. Each creek and groan of the timeworn wood seemed to echo through the centuries as if the very fabric of time held its breath in anticipation of the secrets about to be revealed.

As the last piece of the bookcase was removed and the sealing wax broken, the concealed alcove was revealed. A collective breath escaped the four onlookers as there in the heart of the hidden compartment, lay the skeletal remains of Agnes Thornton.

Jess stepped forward, her eyes welling with tears as she recounted the horrendous act of violence that poor Agnes had been subjected to.

Amongst the dust and the bones, Frank could make out an object that looked like an old bottle. "May I?" He turned to Jess for confirmation that he could reach in and remove the bottle. "Of course, go ahead" Jess whispered feeling sick but also glad that Agnes's remains and the mystery of her disappearance had been solved and she could finally be laid to rest.

"What is it?" queried Jess as he held the bottle up to the light.

"It's a Witches Bottle," said Frank. "Many people in those times had these hidden in their houses to ward off evil spirits or protect them from a certain spell. Whatever this one was unfortunately didn't save Agnes, but it may well have caused harm to another, or so the legends go." Thomas, having played witness to this extraordinary unveiling, retreated quietly from the cottage, leaving Edward and Jess alone. Frank had gone to call the police about the remains, all of them unsure of the next step.

In the quiet aftermath, they all pondered the significance of their discovery, the bones of Agnes and the witch bottle, symbols of resistance against the oppressive currents of history.

"So, "Jess finally spoke. "Now we know the truth about Agnes and can hopefully lay her to rest, what about Rose? How do we find out what happened to her? I feel this story is still unfinished and the recipe book hasn't fully disclosed all its secrets."

"I agree" Edward picked up the old book. "Why don't you finish the recipe for Malkin Pie, it might be that you see something more especially now we have found Agnes?"

Edward and Jess retreated to the kitchen. Jess wanted to make a start immediately and she couldn't bear to look at the broken bookcase and the grisly remains that lay within.

***

As the Malkin Pie went into the oven, Jess turned to Edward. "Would you mind going over to the barn for me and see what's going on please and I'll just tidy up here?" Edward looked at Jess and smiled "Of course, will you be, ok?" "I'm fine, just need to be alone with my thoughts for 5 minutes" Jess began to tidy up the kitchen and check the pie.

As Edward left the cottage, Jess picked up the old recipe book and turned to the page where the recipe for Malkin Pie was. She was studying it trying to see if there were any words or hints that might bring some clarity. Bella was asleep in the chair. "She's getting so old" Jess thought, "I wonder if I should take her to a vet to check on her."

She heard the ping of her oven timer and went back into the kitchen. As she placed the cooked pie on the table, the air changed and the kitchen slowly faded away, replaced by the damp, stone confines of a 17th-century prison cell.

Rose, accused and condemned, sat in the dim light, her eyes reflecting a mixture of defiance and resignation. The cold unforgiving walls bore witness to the anguish of a woman ensnared by false accusations. Her red hair was dull and disheveled, her hands gripped the iron bars. Shadows played upon her pale face, illuminated by the flickering of a solitary candle. In the darkness of the foul-smelling cell, Rose clutched a piece of parchment.

Jess gasped as she now recognized the piece of parchment was the missing piece of the old recipe book that she had been holding only minutes ago.

Rose was looking through the bars at the sounds that were coming closer. Sounds of footsteps approaching her door...

The vision slowly faded away, leaving Jess with the smell of rotten hay and urine and the vision of a condemned Rose.

***

Bella, having now fulfilled her enigmatic role in the unfolding narrative, left Elders Rest and went to find a secluded spot to rest her weary form. That night she vanished into the twilight, leaving behind the echoes of her silent vigil.

Chapter Twenty Two
1612

Rose's footsteps echoed through the cobblestoned streets of Harrop Fold as she approached the familiar silhouette of the cottage. A foreboding stillness hung in the air, and the shadows seemed to stretch and coil with an unspoken secret. As Rose pushed open the creaking door, a knot tightened in her stomach. The cottage, devoid of the comforting presence of Agnes, felt desolate. The hearth, once ablaze with warmth, now lay dormant, its embers whispering tales of absence.

"Mother?" Rose's voice reverberated through the rooms, but only silence answered. The bedroom with its linen draped bed and herbal scents, yielded no answers. The Kitchen, once alive with the alchemy of healing and the smells of cooking now stood as a testament to solitude. "Bella?" she called. The cat, usually a vigilant guardian, was nowhere to be found. Unease settled over Rose like a shroud as she moved through the familiar spaces searching for any sign of her mother or her elusive feline companion.

Rose's footsteps echoed hollowly as she retraced her steps, still calling for her mother and Bella.

Rose's instincts urged her to leave and return to the safety of the Hall, but a deeper compulsion made her continue the search. She could not find any trace of her mother or the cat, but as she turned to leave, she saw a small stain on the hearth of the fireplace. It was blood…but where had it come from? Was Bella hurt or her mother? Looking desperately around the cottage she stumbled across a small piece of parchment that looked as if it had been ripped from a book and as she put it in her pocket, she never heard the silent screams coming from behind the old bookcase. She had no answers and no one to turn to. With a heavy heart, Rose turned away, leaving behind the unanswered questions that lingered in the air like an unspoken incantation.

***

Back at Harrington Hall, the air was charged with tension. Accusations, fueled by fear and suspicion erupted like a tempest. Lord Harrington cast his gaze upon Rose with a cold detachment when she was brought before him.

"So, you've returned, bearing the shadows of Elders Rest and your mother's curses"? he sneered, his accusation intertwining with the sinister currents of the time. "I have heard all the accusations and I believe that your mother has vanished as only a witch can do. As she is nowhere to be found I hold you entirely responsible for not only the death of my son, but that of the witchfinder who your mother's familiar attacked. You have consorted with the devil and used unlawful potions" Lord Harrington was shouting and the servants behind were all murmuring their agreement.

"But I'm innocent" Rose's voice quivered. She looked at the other servants, people she knew, who she had worked with. "Please you know I am not a witch, nor was my mother. I don't know where she is, but she would never have left without telling me." Rose was crying now.

"Enough. I don't want to listen to it anymore." Lord Harrington stood, towering over a cowering Rose. "By the power invested in me, I pronounce you a Witch and you shall be taken thus hence to Lancaster to be imprisoned there until you face trial."

Rose was shackled in irons and put into a horse and cart where she was then taken on the long road to Lancaster. People lined the street as her cart went past chanting and jeering. She could see Jane amongst the crowd and wondered again why she had turned against her. The journey was long and arduous. She was hungry and exhausted and fearful of what lay ahead. On arrival at Lancaster Castle Rose was taken to the Well Tower and put in one of the stone flagged dungeons.

There was nothing Rose could do or say and her friends and neighbours had turned against her. She had lost her mother, her cat, and now her freedom. The damp, stone walls of Rose's cell seemed to absorb what little light penetrated the narrow window, casting a pallid hue upon the desolate chamber. The air, thick with a musty scent, hung stagnant, carrying the weight of centuries old secrets that clung to the rough hew surfaces.

A solitary cot, its wooden frame weathered by time, occupied one corner, its thin mattress offering little reprieve from the unforgiving cold. Faint echoes of distant footsteps reverberated through the corridor outside, a haunting reminder of a world beyond the confines of the cell. A single candle flickered on a crude wooden table, its feeble flame offering scant illumination to the confines of the cell. In the stillness, Rose could hear the distant howl of the wind, a plaintive cry that echoed her own silent lament. The straw-strewn floor beneath her worn boots crunched softly, a reminder of the stark reality she now inhabited.

The barred window, a mere slit in the stone, offered a narrow view of a world that had forsaken her. Beyond the confines of the cell, Lancashire's landscape remained obscured, veiled by the cloak of nightfall. Rose imprisoned within the cell, closed her eyes. In the silence, she could almost hear the whispers of Elders Rest, a spectral chorus that lamented the unjust fate that had befallen both mother and daughter.

The day of reckoning dawned, heralded by the clamour of iron keys and the creaking of heavy doors. Rose clad in tattered garments was escorted through the dimly lit corridors of the prison. The air itself seemed charged with the weight of impending judgement.

Lord Harrington, his face etched with severity, addressed the gathered villagers and other members of the Court. "Rose stands accused of consorting with dark forces, of meddling in the forbidden arts," he declared, casting a shadow over the proceedings. Rose standing in the dock, faced the accusation with a mix of defiance and fear.

"You are charged with the murder of my stillborn son," Lord Harrington continued, "you are also charged with the murder of one David Walker, a witchfinder whom you killed through the evil powers of witchcraft using your familiar, a black cat, and through powers you possess from consorting with the devil. It is also believed that you were instrumental in the disappearance of your own mother, herself a worshipper of the devil "he concluded to the shock of the whole courtroom. "Look everyone, look at her eyes. They are different colours, a sign of the devil's meddling. The mark of witchcraft, there is no doubt".

Villagers stepped forward one by one, their faces a mosaic of suspicion and dread. Their testimonies painted a damning picture of Rose, detailing strange occurrences and inexplicable ailments. Lady Evelyn Harrington was present, seated in the front row and she gazed at Rose with disdain, her belief in the accusations apparent.

Rose, her voice unwavering, addressed the accusations. "I am no witch, and neither was my mother. She was a healer, and a midwife and only tried to help Lady Harrington. I don't know where she is and I beg you to believe me, I am innocent of all those charges." She pleaded as she implored the villagers to see beyond the veil of superstition.

In the hushed courtroom, Margaret, Lady Harrington's loyal maid, found herself torn between duty and compassion. The trial of Rose, accused of witchcraft, was unfolding with an ominous air. As testimonies painted a dark portrait, Margaret felt a surge of empathy for the accused and her missing mother, Agnes. Margaret, standing discreetly near Lady Harrington, wrestled with her conscience. Rose had been a kind soul, often helping her with household chores and Agnes had tended to her ailments with herbal remedies.

Despite the air of accusation, Margaret could not reconcile the benevolent woman she knew with the alleged Witch in the dock. Then when the accusations grew more damning, Margaret could no longer remain a passive spectator. She stood up and began to speak, at first timid but gaining courage.

. "My Lord, she implored, her voice wavering with conviction, "Rose and Agnes are good women. They've done no harm. I don't know what has happened to Agnes but she would never leave her daughter and Rose would never harm her."

Lord Harrington, however, dismissed Margaret's plea, refusing to entertain dissent. "It is obvious looking at her, with her marks of the devil that she is a witch. She used her powers to make her mother disappear. Together with her familiar, she cursed the Witchfinder David Walker until he suffered an agonizing death, and don't forget she gave Lady Harrington a potion which killed my son and heir."

Unable to contain herself, Margaret shouted "You're wrong! These accusations are baseless" she exclaimed, her words cutting through the tense atmosphere. Villagers exchanged glances, uncertain how to react to a servant speaking against Lord Harrington.

Lord Harrington looked to the judge and with a nod of his head, the judge ordered Margaret's removal from the court. "Silence, simpleton! Your words hold no weight here," he declared. As Margaret was escorted out, her pleas echoed in the minds of those who witnessed the unexpected defiance.

Suddenly, from the back of the courtroom, Jane stood up. She cleared her throat and began to speak, her voice wavering slightly with emotion.

"Your Honors" she started addressing the judge and Lord Harrington. "I have witnessed things in this household that cannot be explained by natural means. Strange occurrences and unexplained happenings that have left me fearful for my life." "Livestock have been struck down as well as a servant in the very kitchen where I work. Who else could be responsible but Rose for these wicked deeds?" Jane continued, her voice rising with conviction. "She has always been a strange one, with her peculiar eyes and her mother Agnes was well known for her potion making. I have even seen them together, plotting and scheming." She finished gloatingly.

The courtroom erupted into murmurs and whispers as Jane's words hung in the air.

She could see the fear and uncertainty in Rose's eyes, and a cruel satisfaction twisted in her gut as she realized the power she finally held in her hands.

***

The judge, a stern-faced elder, pronounced the verdict. "Guilty" … Thou shalt not suffer a witch to live, you will be hanged by the neck until you are dead."

In a cruel twist of fate, the gavel fell sealing Rose's destiny. Sentenced to hang for crimes that never existed, she was escorted back to the cold solitude of her cell. The gallows looming on the horizon cast a foreboding silhouette against the Lancashire sky.

Jane returned from the court with the other villagers who had been witnesses and then returned to the hall on foot. She was delighted with the outcome of the trial and hoped that now Lord and Lady Harrington might reward her for her words. She felt no guilt about her part in poor Lady Harrington's stillborn child and rejoiced that Rose had suffered the consequences of her actions.

As she made her way back to the hall her path intersected with a grazing pasture where the estate's cows roamed freely. Unbeknownst to her, Bella lurked nearby. The cat's presence disturbed the placid tranquility of the grazing animals as she crept stealthily between them. She meowed and hissed running between the legs of the cows, her movements startling a scream of swifts who rose up in a cloud of feathers and the high "shree" sound they made which reverberated across the pasture in a scream.

Suddenly, startled, the cattle began to stampede in a frenzy of panic. Jane rushed over to the wall by the edge of the field intending to climb over. The cows, their thunderous hooves trampling everything in their path headed towards her, and in the chaos that ensued Jane found herself caught amid the tumult. She tried in vain to climb the wall but the herd was frightened by the cat and the birds, heedless in their stampede, crushing her against the wall. Her cries were drowned out by the deafening cacophony of hooves and bellows. Her broken and trampled body was found some days later by the estate workers, crushed and lifeless against the old stone wall.

Chapter Twenty Three
One Year Later

As the newly renovated café buzzed with activity, Jess couldn't help but feel a sense of pride and satisfaction. The place was bustling with customers, the aroma of freshly brewed coffee and baked goods filling the air. She had poured her heart and soul into turning the old barn into a thriving business, and seeing it come to life was a dream come true. She had called the café "The Witches Brew". The old barn was completely transformed. The old door had been replaced by glass and the hayloft was made into a mezzanine floor also with large glass windows that meant visitors to the café could see all around them with the most amazing views of the surrounding countryside. The mezzanine floor was a lovely space with comfy sofas and cushions where clients could relax and enjoy the views, whilst the main space downstairs was all polished wooden floors, with locally sourced mismatched tables and chairs, cauldron-shaped hanging baskets with overflowing trailing ivy and candles on all the tables. The original old recipe book had been framed and took pride of place behind the counter. Philip, now fully recovered, had given Jess a lovely old grandfather clock that stood in the corner and had helped her source a wonderful old chandelier that hung from the centre of the ceiling.

She offered a varied menu but had stuck to her original plan of offering traditional Lancashire recipes, especially pies and baked goods. She had also just perfected a recipe for Rowan Berry Jelly, which she had called "Bella's Berry Compote" (+) and it was proving a big seller. It was great on cheese on toast, but Jess liked to use it traditionally with steak, chops, or beef and always added it to her slow-cooked lamb. Adeline, who was a skilled seamstress, had made all the chair covers, curtains, and tablecloths, and Melissa, had helped her source a local artist and she had his paintings on the walls. She had found a lovely young couple from Clitheroe, James David (or JD as he liked to be called) who was helping her in the kitchen and the bakery and was already showing signs of becoming a talented chef, and Carys who waited on the tables and was very popular with clients because of her sunny disposition and friendly chatter.

The previous year Jess had discovered Bella who had disappeared suddenly, underneath the ancient Rowan tree in the field opposite the barn, beneath the dappled sunlight. The large tree, according to Frank, always lost its leaves before any other tree and was always the first to regain its leaves in Spring. The Rowan was known in local folklore to protect against witchcraft and enchantment and often known as a Faerie tree because of its abundance of white flowers. It also produced red berries, each berry having a five pointed star opposite its stalk. Agnes's remains had been handed back to Jess and Edward and they joined forces to give them both the rest they deserved. Jess felt a bittersweet solace in uniting the spirits of both Agnes and Bella beneath the sheltering branches of the mystical Rowan Tree.

During the renovation of the barn, they discovered two little kittens, one black and one ginger. They had enquired locally but no one was missing any kittens and no mother appeared to be around, so they decided to keep them. They missed Bella and enjoyed having the kittens around. The cats loved Elders Rest and would come into the café too, which the customers loved. Jess had called them Pandora and Walter and they in turn loved Jess and Edward and were very loving, although mischievous too. The black kitten,

Pandora, had eyes that were a bright green, whilst Walter's were an unusual golden brown.

They had never found any records of Rose's death or any clue as to what became of her but through some old records in the library there was a note of the death of a David Walker, who had died suddenly due to a Witches curse.

The Witches Brew Café had generated a lot of interest in the surrounding villages and some of Jess's recipes had become very popular. She had recently made a new recipe for Curried Chicken Pie (+) as she wanted to update her recipes not just use the old Lancashire ones.

As she was making the pie that day, she thought back to what Frank had told her that morning. There was an old lady in one of the local care homes who had heard about the café and Elders Rest and the remains that were found there. She had asked Frank to tell Jess to come and see her as she had something she wanted to give to her. Jess couldn't possibly think what it could be but was intrigued and was going later that morning. The old lady's name was June Thornton.

***

The Manor House Nursing Home was in the village of Chatburn. Jess rang the bell and was ushered into a large sitting area where residents were relaxing watching the television or playing cards and for those that wanted to join in there was a quiz underway. She enquired about June who wasn't in the lounge but in her room. She made her way down the hallway, her footsteps echoing softly against the tiled floor. At the end of the hall, she found June Thornton's room, the door slightly ajar.

"June?" Jess called softly as she pushed the door open, peering inside. The room was small but full of furniture, lamps, and photos, the afternoon sunlight streaming in through the window.

"Come in dear, don't be shy" June's voice called from the bed, her frail form propped up by pillows. She smiled warmly as Jess approached, her eyes bright despite her fragility.

"I heard about you through Frank, he comes to visit you know. He told me about you finding the remains of poor Agnes."

Jess looked at the old lady, "Yes it was sad but at least she is now at rest."

"I know and I thank you for that. My family lived in Harrop Fold for many years and for a time at Elders Rest, my dear." Jess was amazed "Really, I never knew". Curious Jess watched as June reached for a small wooden chest on the bedside table. With trembling hands, she opened it, revealing a weathered old diary nestled inside.

"This belonged to Rose" June explained her voice tinged with emotion. "She wrote it while she was imprisoned, detailing her thoughts and feelings during those dark days."

"How do you have it in your possession? if you don't mind me asking "Jess was amazed, curious, and excited.

"It's been in my family for generations, we were ancestors of Anges Thornton but until today I didn't know who would be interested in it, but I feel after speaking with Frank, it is only right you should read it, my dear."

Jess's heart skipped a beat as she reached for the diary, her fingers trembling with anticipation. She flipped through the pages, her eyes scanning the faded ink.

"It's incredible" Jess murmured, her voice barely above a whisper. "To think that Rose poured her heart and soul into these pages, knowing that she would never see the outside world again."

June nodded, her eyes misting over with tears. "She was a strong woman, Rose. She said softly "And I believe her story deserves to be told."

"Thank you, June, Jess said her voice choked with emotion. "For entrusting me with this precious piece of history. I promise to honour Rose's memory and ensure that her story is never forgotten."

"I know you will my dear and having met with you I can't think of anyone better to carry on her legacy."

As Jess left the Manor House Nursing Home, she couldn't wait to get home and read the diary with Edward.

Chapter Twenty Four
Excerpt from Rose's Diary

Day 56:
The days blur together now, each one melting into the next like wax dripping from my only candle. I find solace in these pages, the only refuge left to me in this cold, dank cell. My thoughts constantly drift to happier times, to the laughter and warmth of my home Elders Rest, now just a distant memory.

Day 63:
They came for me today, their footsteps echoing like the tolling of a death knell. I stood tall, my chin held high, refusing to let them see the fear that gnaws at my insides. But as they dragged me from my cell, my resolve wavered, and I found myself trembling like a leaf in the wind.

Day 64:
The trial was a mockery of justice, a farce played out on a stage soaked in blood and tears. They accused me of crimes I did not commit. There was only one, Margaret, who tried to defend me, but the damning lies of Jane were the only words heard. I felt the weight of prejudice and fear bearing down on me, crushing me beneath its heel.

Day 65:
They say that tomorrow will be my last, that I will meet my end at the gallows as a witch condemned. But I am not afraid, for I know that my soul will soar free from this earthly prison, unfettered by the chains of hatred and ignorance that bind me here.

Day 66:
As I await the dawn, I find comfort in these final moments, knowing that I will be reunited with those I have lost, even though I still know not of the fate of my beloved mother Agnes. My only other regret is that I will never see the sunrise again, its golden rays warming my face and filling my heart with hope. But my mother always told me that even in the darkest hour, there is light to be found, if only we dare to seek it.

THE END

Epilogue

Later that year in the glow of lantern light and the warmth of their friends and neighbours, Jess and Edward exchanged their vows within the walls of the renovated barn. Their union was a celebration of love triumphing over the shadows that clung to Elders Rest and marked the dawn of a new chapter.

The café, once a dormant space, awakened to the aroma of freshly brewed coffee and the delicious smells of pies baking in the ovens. When Jess and Edward opened its doors, they felt the presence of those who had shaped its history. The café and Elders Rest now stood as a beacon of resilience and rebirth.

The sun dipped below the horizon, casting a golden glow over the hamlet of Harrop
Fold, and for a moment all was quiet and still.

Yet, even as the future beckoned, the specter of the past still lingered. In a quiet moment, Jess found herself gazing out over the fells which were bathed in ethereal light. There, beneath the watchful eye of Pendle Hill, a faint shadow flickered, a fleeting glimpse of Rose, forever entwined with the untold tales that danced in the gentle whispers of the Lancashire Winds.

***

As the two kittens curled up together nestled in the warmth of Elders Rest, they drifted into slumber, guarding the secrets of the past and the promises of the future.... Each kitten slept as always, with one eye open.

RECIPES

Lancashire Cheese and Onion Pie.

Ingredients:
Pastry
9oz All-purpose Flour
5oz Butter
2 Egg Yolks
Cold Water

Filling
1oz butter
3 onions
10oz Lancashire cheese coarsely grated.
Cold Water
Loose bottomed tart tin approx. 20cm wide and 4cm deep.

Method

Make the pastry. Combine the flour and the butter until it resembles fine breadcrumbs. Add the two egg yolks (save the white of the eggs for your egg wash later)

Option: here you can add salt and pepper (I use white pepper for this recipe) or even some paprika or chilli if you want to make it a bit spicy)

Add ice cold water until it comes together as a dough.

Wrap in cling film and chill in the fridge. (I always make my pastry the day before so it is in the fridge overnight) make sure you chill for at least 30 minutes.

Make the filling.

Put the thinly sliced onions in a pan with the butter and water. Boil then simmer until they are soft and translucent. Grate the cheese whilst the onions cool. Drain any water off the onions.

Grease your tin and roll out your pastry, putting the bottom ring of pastry in the base of your dish. Gently brush some egg wash around the edges.

Layer your onions and cheese until the pie dish is almost full. Here you can add more pepper if you want. I always add a dash of

Worcestershire sauce but again that's optional.

Place your pastry lid on and seal. Decorate as you wish and use the remaining egg white to glaze.

Place in the oven gas mark 180 for approx. 25 minutes or until the filling is oozing slightly. Enjoy!!

Malkin Pie (Agnes's version of …)

Ingredients:

For the spiced Chutney Base:

1 cup of mango chutney
1 teaspoon ground cumin
1 teaspoon ground coriander
½ teaspoon chilli powder
Salt and pepper to taste

For the lamb layer:

1 pound of lamb, diced or minced
2 tablespoons olive oil
2 cloves of garlic, minced or crushed
1 teaspoon ground cumin
1 teaspoon smoked paprika
Dash of Lancashire Sauce (can be found in local delicatessen)

Salt & pepper to taste

For the Vegetable layer:

1 cup of carrots finely chopped
1 cup of peas
2 potatoes finely chopped
1 tablespoon of butter
Salt and pepper to taste

For the Steak Layer:

1 pound of best steak (sirloin or ribeye)
1 tablespoon of olive oil
1 teaspoon of dried thyme
Dash of red wine
Salt and pepper to taste

For the Bacon layer:

8 slices of bacon, cooked and crumbled

For the pie crust:

2 sheets of short crust pastry as per the cheese and onion pie but infuse the pastry with some more dried thyme and garlic salt.

Instructions:

Pre heat your oven to 190
Chill your pastry

Prepare the spiced chutney:
In a bowl mix together the mango chutney, ground cumin, coriander, chilli powder and salt and pepper, set aside.

Cook the lamb:
Heat olive oil, add minced garlic and the lamb.
Season with cumin, paprika salt and pepper.
Cook until the lamb is brown and add your Lancashire sauce to taste.
Set it aside.

Prepare the vegetables:
Cook diced carrots, peas and potatoes in butter until softened and season with salt and pepper.
Cook the steak:
In the same pan used for the lamb, add olive oil. Cook the thinly sliced steak with dried thyme, salt and pepper until browned and add the red wine to taste.

Assemble the pie:

Roll out one sheet of pastry and line a pie dish with it.
Spread a layer of the spiced chutney on the bottom.
Layer the lamb, followed by the cooked vegetables, sliced steak and finally the crumbled bacon.

Roll out the second sheet of pastry and place it on top of the pie. Seal the edges and brush the top with beaten egg for a golden finish. Decorate as you wish.

Bake in the oven for 30 mins or until the pastry is golden brown and cooked through.

Enjoy your creation!

Hindle Wakes

Ingredients

One whole chicken
Juice of two lemons
Bisto or other gravy mix
1lb of prunes

Method:

Wash the lemon, pare the rind thinly and simmer it gently in one pint of water for 15 minutes to extract the flavour.

Add to this water the strained juice of the two lemons.

Wash the prunes and pour over the lemon water and let them soak overnight.

Stuff the chicken with the prunes and steam for 6 hours or more till tender.

Wrap the chicken in bacon fastened with a skewer and roast for one hour or until cooked through and golden.

Serve with good brown gravy, using any of the lemon liquid that was not soaked up. (Or any version of a good gravy would be fine.)

Enjoy!!

Lancashire Foots

For the pastry
850g Plain Flour
2 Egg Yolks, beaten
140g Lard
140g Butter
200ml Milk
200ml Water
½ tsp salt
1/2tsp ground black pepper

For the filling

200g Lancashire Cheese
200g Thick slices of bacon (fried and allowed to cool)
200g boiled ham
1 onion, peeled and finely chopped
1tbsp butter

1tsp salt
1tsp black pepper
1tsp English Mustard Powder
1 egg beaten to glaze
2 tbsp milk to seal the pasties.

Method:

Pastry

In a bowl sieve the flour and sprinkle in salt and pepper. Make a well in the centre.
In a saucepan gently heat the lard and butter in the milk and water until it has melted, then bring rapidly to the boil. Pour the water and dissolved fats into the well in the flour and mix with a wooden spoon. Add the beaten egg yolks to form a dough. Cover leave to rest for 30 mins then put into the fridge to chill for. 2 hours.

Making the Foots
Fry the bacon in a frying pan with the butter and when cool cut into small dice and put them in a mixing bowl. Chop up the cheese and boiled ham and mix with the bacon. In the same pan fry the onions and when cool add to the bowl with the bacon, cheese and ham. Mix with the salt, pepper and mustard powder.

We will be making two shapes out of the pastry, hence the name "Foots" (never feet).

Roll out the pastry on a lightly floured surface to form a large oval shape about 1cm thick. Cut in half lengthwise and separate the two pastry pieces.

Take each piece of pastry and turn it around so the cut long side is away from you. Using a rolling pin across the middle of each one, roll away from you to make another oval shape. This will leave half of the pastry nearest you still thick (the heel) and half the pastry wider and thinner (the sole).

Preheat oven to 190C

Brush all around the edges of the "foots" with milk to seal. Take half of the filling and put it in the centre of the thicker heel. Turn the thinner soles over to enclose the filling, sealing the edges well. Place the "foots" on a greased baking sheet. Brush all over the tops with beaten egg to glaze. Bake for 30 mins or until golden brown.

You can serve Lancashire Foots either warm or cold.

Enjoy!

Steak and Stilton Pie (The author's recipe)

Ingredients
Two onions
10 oz braising steak (fat removed)
One pint of Beef Stock
Worcestershire Sauce (dash)
Red Wine (tbsp)
Dried thyme (to taste)
Salt and Pepper
Stilton Cheese

Pastry
Shortcrust recipe as for the cheese and onion pie, adding some dried thyme to the mix.

Method

I always use my slow cooker for this recipe. Put the steak, onions, stock, Worcestershire sauce, red wine and thyme and salt and pepper in your slow cooker. Cook for at least 5 hours until the meat falls apart. Leave to cool. If the gravy is too thin add corn flour and water mix to thicken.

Line your pie dish with one disk of pastry then put the cooled filling in. Sprinkle over the crumbled stilton cheese and more black pepper.

Cover with your other half of pastry and seal. Decorate as you wish. Bake in the oven (190C) for approx. 25 to 30 mins or until golden brown.

Enjoy! It will smell and taste delicious.

Parkin Recipe

8oz fine or medium oatmeal
8oz self-raising flour
80z brown sugar
Salt
2tsp ground ginger
225g butter
125g black treacle
125g syrup
1 egg beaten.

Method

Put oatmeal, flour, sugar, salt and ginger in a bowl. Mix it all together.
Rub in the fat.
When it's all mixed in add the treacle, golden syrup and egg.
Mix well. This will make the mixture quite heavy.
Place in a lined, roasting tin (Loaf tin)
Cook at 150-170C for 1 to 1 and a half hours.

Leave in tin for approximately 4 days before digging in.

Enjoy!

Tharf Cake (biscuits)

Ingredients

230g each of oatmeal, self-raising flour and sugar
170 g black treacle
170g butter
30g candied peel1tsp baking powder.
Pinch of ground ginger, salt and coriander seeds.

Method

Grease a baking tray.
Rub the butter into the dry ingredients and add the warmed treacle.
Knead lightly before rolling out and cutting into thin rounds.
Bake for about 10 minutes at 190C until golden brown.
Leave to cool or enjoy warm.

Enjoy!

CURRIED CHICKEN PIE

Ingredients:

100ml thick yoghurt
Juice of one lemon
1tbsp curry powder
800g boneless chicken breast
One large onion
15g root ginger peeled and chopped.
Four cloves of garlic
1 tbsp olive oil
1tsp turmeric
1 tbsp tomato puree
Handful of chopped coriander
450g spinach
30 g ground almonds
One chilli chopped.
Salt and pepper

Pastry as in the other recipes

Method:

Make your pastry (add turmeric to the mix if desired)
Chill in the fridge for at least 2 hours or overnight.

Dice the chicken breast and marinate in the yoghurt, lemon juice and curry powder.

Cook the onion, garlic, ginger, chilli, and turmeric until translucent.
Add the tomato puree.
Add the chicken mixture and cook until chicken tender. Add water if necessary.
Add the ground almonds.
Add the spinach and coriander and cook for at least 40 mins.

Place your base disc of pastry in the pie dish. Option here to add a layer of mango chutney onto the base (highly recommend)

Place cooled chicken curry mixture into dish and cover with remaining pasty. Brush with egg yolk or white (saved from pastry) to seal.

Decorate as you wish and (option here to glaze pastry with lime pickle).

Bake in oven for 25-30 mins at 190C.

Enjoy (it is delicious hot or cold).

BELLA'S BERRY COMPOTE (Rowan Berry Jelly)

Ingredients

1.5kg rowan berries
1.5kg crab apples
450g white sugar
Juice of one lemon
(Some fresh rosemary -optional)

Method

Chop apples and put into a large heavy saucepan with the rowan berries.
Just cover the fruits with water and bring to the boil. Turn the heat down and simmer until the fruits are soft and broken down, approx. 20 mins.

Lay a muslin cloth over a large bowl and tip the fruits and liquid into the cloth and gather the edges together.

Tie the cloth above the bowl and suspend from a chair, table, or beam.

Allow the liquid to drip into the bowl for a least 4 hours or overnight.

Measure the juice in a jug then pour into the pan. For every 600ml of fluid add 450g sugar. Add the lemon juice and bring to the boil.

Boil rapidly for 10 minutes and then test for setting point. Once your jelly has reached setting point take off the heat, pour into clean sterilised jars and seal.

This jelly is great for jazzing up cheese on toast or used traditionally with steak, chops, roast beef, or chicken. It is also great added to slow-cooked lamb.

Enjoy!

Extras (Just for fun). As cooked by Mrs Higgins.

Roasted Sparrows

Sparrows were plucked and then singed slightly over a flame to remove any feathers or hairs and then roasted in the oven with butter, thyme, rosemary, and salt. Sparrows are a useful source of protein and other nutrients.! Personally, I would use Poussin!!

<u>Lamprey Pie</u>

Ingredients

1lb Lampreys (an eel like fish, not to everyone's taste! See alternatives below).
1lb of puff pastry
1 onion finely chopped.
2 cloves of garlic minced.
1 tbs butter
Salt and pepper to taste
A pinch of ground cloves

A pinch of ground mace
A pinch of nutmeg
A splash of red wine

Method

Clean the lampreys removing skin and any undesirable parts.
In a pan melt the butter and sauté the chopped onion and garlic until softened.
Add the cleaned lampreys to the pan and cook for a few minutes.
Season with the herbs and red wine.
Line a pie dish with the pastry and arrange the lampreys inside.
Cover with puff pastry lid making a small hole in the centre.
Bake in the oven at 190c for about 45 minutes.

You could substitute Lampreys for Salmon or Trout.

Enjoy!

Pobs and Pobbies

When bread was about a day old it would be broken into chunks and put in a cup with warmed milk and sugar.

Lobs and Lobbies

If there were any meat juices off any meat that was eaten, chunks of bread would be placed in a cup and the meat juices poured over.

If bread soaked in meat juices are eaten as a sandwich and not in a cup they are known as Dip Butties. Yum!!

And finally, just because I like the name:

Wet Nelly

This was a Lancashire dessert that resembles a bread pudding. It was made by soaking bread in milk or cream, sweetening it with sugar and adding dried fruits and spices. The result is a moist indulgent treat that warms the heart.

About the Author

This is the first novel by Juliet Carolan. Juliet has lived in Lancashire all her life and loves the countryside and the cuisine. She has had a varied career over the years and has been and still is an avid reader. She is now retired and living in Vietnam with her husband and living there has given her the time and inspiration to start writing. She has one son, Oliver, who still lives in Lancashire.

Juliet grew up with tales of the Pendle Witches which inspired this novel, alongside living in the lovely hamlet of Harrop Fold where this novel is based. Although Elders Rest is fictional, she did live in Manor House Cottage in the hamlet which provided the idea for the story. She is currently working on her second novel **Footsteps of Fate**, which is also based in Lancashire, and is a haunting tale of love and loss written over two time periods covering Edwardian England and the present time. Part of the story is also set in Greece, on the island of Crete in a little village called Elounda which holds an incredibly special place in the author's heart.

Printed in Great Britain
by Amazon